# IMPROMPTU IN MORIBUNDIA

BY PATRICK HAMILTON

FICTION

*Monday Morning*
*Craven House*
*Twopence Coloured*
*Twenty Thousand Streets Under the Sky*
*Impromptu in Moribundia*
*Hangover Square*
*The Slaves of Solitude*
*The West Pier*
*Mr Simpson and Mr Gorse*
*Unknown Assailant*

PLAYS

*Rope*
*John Brown's Body*
*Gaslight*
*Money with Menaces*
*To the Public Danger*
*The Duke in Darkness*
*The Man Upstairs*

# PATRICK HAMILTON

# IMPROMPTU IN MORIBUNDIA

ABACUS

First published in Great Britain in 1939 by Constable
This paperback edition published in 2018 by Abacus

1 3 5 7 9 10 8 6 4 2

A CIP catalogue record for this book
is available from the British Library.

ISBN 978-0-349-14162-6

Typeset in Sabon by M Rules
Printed and bound in Great Britain by
Clays Ltd, Elcograf S.p.A.

Papers used by Abacus are from well-managed forests
and other responsible sources.

Abacus
An imprint of
Little, Brown Book Group
Carmelite House
50 Victoria Embankment
London EC4Y 0DZ

An Hachette UK Company
www.hachette.co.uk

www.littlebrown.co.uk

# INTRODUCTION

It is a mystery that for many years the work of one of the century's most darkly hilarious and penetrating artists fell into near obscurity. Doris Lessing declared: 'I am continually amazed that there is a kind of roll call of OK names from the 1930s . . . Auden, Isherwood etc. But Hamilton is never on them and he is a much better writer than any of them'.

Recently, however, Hamilton's novel *The Slaves of Solitude* was adapted for the stage, and the films of his taut thrillers, *Gaslight* and Alfred Hitchcock's adaptation of *Rope* are now considered classics. He is regularly championed by contemporary writers such as Sarah Waters, Dan Rhodes and Will Self.

Patrick Hamilton was one of the most gifted and admired writers of his generation. With a father who made an excellent prototype for the bombastic bullies of his later novels and a snobbish mother who alternately neglected and smothered him, Hamilton was born into Edwardian gentility in Hassocks, Sussex, in 1904. He and his parents moved a short while later to Hove, where he spent his early years. He became a keen observer of the English boarding house, the twilit world of pubs and London backstreets and of the quiet desperation of everyday life. But after gaining acclaim and prosperity through his early work, Hamilton's morale was shattered when a road accident left him disfigured and an already sensitive nature turned towards morbidity.

Hamilton's personality was plagued by contradictions. He played the West End clubman and the low-life bohemian. He sought, with sometimes menacing zeal, his 'ideal woman' and then would indulge with equal intensity his sadomasochistic obsessions among prostitutes. He was an ideological Marxist who in later years reverted to blimpish Toryism. Two successive wives, who catered to contradictory demands, shuttled him back and forth. Through his work run the themes of revenge and punishment, torturer and victim; yet there is also a compassion and humanity which frequently produces high comedy.

In the 1930s and 40s, despite personal setbacks and an increasing problem with drink, Hamilton was able to write some of his best work. His novels include the masterpiece *Hangover Square*, *The Midnight Bell*, *The Plains of Cement*, *The Siege of Pleasure*, a trilogy entitled *Twenty Thousand Streets Under the Sky* and The Gorse Trilogy, made up of *The West Pier*, *Mr Stimpson and Mr Gorse* and *Unknown Assailant*.

*Impromptu in Moribundia* is something of an anomaly in Hamilton's career – and by far his most overtly political novel. Its protagonist John Sadler is transported by a futuristic machine to Moribundia, an uncanny world which partly resembles 1930s London. Viewed from a certain angle, Moribundia is the definitive communist fantasy, free from the tyranny of wage labour. Yet its society is staunchly materialistic: worshipping cleanliness, helpless in the face of illness. A woman buys a new brand of soap and transforms from a gawky spinster into a sought-after beauty. The protagonist catches measles and a doctor declares him near death.

As a critique of consumerism and class, *Impromptu* places Hamilton within a tradition of English satirists such as Aldous Huxley, who interpreted the hypocrisies around them through allegory and dystopia. But unlike *Brave New Word*, Moribundia – with its radical reimagining of worker's pay and leisurely working-class – is not a straightforward dystopia. It is contradictory, and gloriously irresolute.

J. B. Priestley described Hamilton as 'uniquely individual ... he is the novelist of innocence, appallingly vulnerable, and of malevolence, coming out of some mysterious darkness of evil.' Patrick Hamilton died in 1962.

# IMPROMPTU IN
# MORIBUNDIA

'... the universe begins to look more like a great thought than like a great machine. Mind no longer appears as an accidental intruder in the realm of matter; we are beginning to suspect that we ought rather to hail it as the creator and governor of the realm of matter ...'

SIR JAMES JEANS, *The Mysterious Universe*

There's a breathless hush in the Close to-night –
Ten to make and the match to win –
A bumping pitch and a blinding light,
An hour to play and the last man in.
And it's not for the sake of a ribboned coat,
Or the selfish hope of a season's fame,
But his Captain's hand on his shoulder smote –
'Play up! play up! and play the game!'

SIR HENRY NEWBOLT

# CHAPTER ONE

It is now generally known that, after the general controversy and outburst attendant upon John Sadler's initial heroic journey to another planet, and later the partially fruitless attempt of the Gosling brothers, it had been decided by Crowmarsh to keep my departure hidden from the press and unknown to the general public. This was as much for Crowmarsh's own personal safety as for reasons of scientific detachment. Only five weeks ago he had been assaulted savagely in the street by three prejudiced and self-righteous gentlemen, who escaped with nothing worse than a small fine, and it was generally felt that if the actual whereabouts of his *Asteradio* had been known widely, it would have been smashed to small pieces by his enemies in a few days' time. Not that that would have seriously damaged Abel Crowmarsh. It is now well known that the wonder and terror of his epoch-making instrument is only equalled by its extreme comparative simplicity of construction. The only expedient left would have been to smash Abel Crowmarsh himself to small pieces along with his machine, and even that would have been of little avail. His assistants and associates, armed with a fanatical zeal greater even than that of their opponents, now have the knowledge, skill and means to gain the day against the destroyers even if they have the whole opinion of the world on their side. The *Asteradio* is with us now, and that is the end of the matter.

It was, then, only Crowmarsh himself, a few of his assistants, and one or two personal friends of my own, who knew of my departure at all, and so I was deprived of any of the glory and embarrassment of a public 'send-off.' A little dinner was given to me the night before by those few friends, and that was all. Offers were indeed made to come round and accompany me to what was facetiously called my 'execution' in the morning, but I firmly declined them. I never could stand anything in the nature of 'seeing-off' – a prejudice originally acquired from hideous experiences on Victoria Station in the war of 1914.

I returned that night to my rooms in New Cavendish Street, a little drunk, I think, and with a well-nourished sense of high adventure just holding its own against a lurking feeling of sheer panic which urged me to back out gracefully, or, if that was impossible, to run away. I slept well. When I awoke, at half-past seven, I need hardly say that all that sense of high adventure had departed. On the other hand, the feeling of sheer panic had not, as yet at any rate, seized the territory evacuated by the other emotion. I should say my sensations were those of fright, certainly – but of a sort of numbed fright, not of panic. A beastly feeling enough, for all that.

My early morning cup of tea was brought me, and I smoked a cigarette. My blinds had not been pulled up, but I could see that it was a fine warm day outside. For some reason that fact in itself seemed strangely to disquiet me – to this day I hardly know why. Perhaps it was the thought of the blue sky – the clear, pellucid nakedness of the infinite space into which I was to be hurled! I got up quickly, drew the blinds, looked squarely and defiantly into the cloudless sky, went and had my bath, and shaved. I cut myself slightly while shaving, but this was not because my hand was trembling. It was quite firm. I remember I had a feeling of dreadful unreality as I looked at myself closely in the mirror.

I can only describe my sensations up to this time as similar

to those of a man about to undergo a major operation in a few
hours' time – a man, that is, walking about and feeling perfectly
well at the moment, and therefore deprived of the motive and
stimulus of physical pain in throwing himself upon his fate. But
when my breakfast came matters grew speedily worse. What was
all this? Baths, shavings, breakfasts! – and in a few hours' time
I was to be on another planet! I looked at the clock with terror
and appeal in my eyes. Good God. I had exactly an hour and a
half! I tried to eat my breakfast, but, of course, the first mouthful
stuck in my mouth, and, finding myself, after laborious chewing,
absolutely incapable of performing the act of swallowing, I had
to spit it out. Instead I managed to gulp down some coffee, and
greedily lit another cigarette. I spent the next half-hour pacing
up and down my room and smoking, and I shall never forget the
smell and the taste of the coffee, the filthy spectacle of the uneaten
breakfast, and the slow-curling wreaths and great banks of blue
smoke in the blinding sunshine coming through the window.

It had been my intention to take a taxi round to Crowmarsh,
which would have only taken me ten minutes at the most; but I
was so wrought up that I decided to walk.

If any one of my readers has ever gone through the experience
of fainting, or of thinking he was about to faint, in a public place,
he will be able more readily to appreciate the sort of feeling I
had as I got out in the air that morning and started walking.
I do not mean that I was fainting, or even that I thought I was
going to faint, but the whole world bore the demeanour it bears
to the fainting man – that is to say it seemed to be, simultaneously, both far away and near, at once confused and remote, yet
agonizingly real and urgent, terribly quiet, yet terribly noisy,
floating away, and yet coming in upon him and filling his ears
with an awful hubbub. Above all, the things and people moving

about in this world assume a character of cold indifference to
his plight which he can hardly bear; he for a moment loses any
sort of conception that they are ignorant of his sufferings, and
their brutal health and uncomprehending normality have an
air of deliberate disinterest in himself. He envies and bitterly
resents their ability to behave as ordinary human-beings: he is
temporarily, indeed, a complete outcast from the universe itself,
from the whole of life as it is known and lived. That is what I felt
as I walked down New Cavendish Street that warm, brilliantly
sunny September morning. Taxis swished by me, people passed
me laughing on the pavements, the shops were open and lazily
starting the morning's routine, errand boys sped by whistling on
their bicycles, everything and everybody was going forward in a
perfectly orderly and peaceful way and yet in less than an hour's
time I, I out of all these happy absorbed people, would be millions
upon millions of miles up and away in that sky! How could they
remain so aloof, how could they refrain so coolly and obstinately
as they did from looking at me, speaking to me, crowding round
and wondering at me, morally supporting me in some way in my
awful undertaking?

After a few minutes these feelings passed away, or rather were
absorbed again in a general numbness, and I walked ahead at
a steady pace. As is now well known Crowmarsh at that time
worked his miracles in Chandos Street, W.1, and so my route lay
all the way through the stately land of Nursing Homes – New
Cavendish Street, Wimpole Street, Welbeck Street, Harley Street,
Bentinck Street, Devonshire Street and the rest. How few people
realize, strolling in this district in the ordinary way, that under
the aegis of these impressive titles and behind those graceful pros-
perous façades, lie hidden consulting rooms, sick-rooms, X-ray
rooms, operating theatres, doctors, sisters, nurses, anaesthetists,

disinfectants, stretchers, and all the starched hell and paraphernalia of the medical world! The thought came in upon me with great force that morning and gave me a minute measure of comfort. I thought of all those undergoing critical operations, all those to whom, as to me, this morning was a morning of terror and strangeness, of ghastly isolation from the normal world, and who lay in clean (oh, so clean!) white-sheeted suspense for the sound of the trolley in the corridor, the trolley which for all they knew might indeed be wheeling them away from everybody for ever. I told myself that my case was no worse than theirs, that I was merely undergoing a kind of serious operation, and I reminded myself for the thousandth time that the *Asteradio* had succeeded in actually annihilating no one as yet – though I had no desire to share the fate of the younger Gosling brother.

Encouraged by these thoughts I took heart again to look up into the blue sky above, but it would not do, I had to take my eyes away. If only it had been at night, if only the stars were shining and I had been able to see where I was going, to perceive my destination as an actuality, a solid orb, however tiny, occupying its own position in space, I believe I could have faced matters with greater calm – but the horror of being shot up at ten o'clock in the morning into that glaring blue utter nothingness to nowhere visible! One unforgettable night Crowmarsh had actually shown me my destination through the telescope, and I had felt very grand, and audacious, and noble, and unutterably large; but where was it now, and why was I feeling so unutterably small? Had it not vanished altogether, along with my fatuous complacency, and had it indeed any existence save in Crowmarsh's brain? From that moment I had to keep my eyes glued on the pavement in order to get where I was going.

When I reached Chandos Street I saw by my wrist-watch that I was exactly twelve minutes too early. My desire to wander about and delay the moment, my desire to run madly away anywhere and never come back, held a brief combat with my desire to get in anywhere away from that awful blue sky, and the latter prevailed. I went straight up to the house and rang the bell. It differed in no respect from any dentist's or specialist's bell in that district. To go round at ten o'clock in the morning and ring a bell to be sent, please, to a planet nobody could see! Even at that moment I was struck by the staggering irony and absurdity of my situation.

The door was opened by the famous and incongruous Albert Fry, that curious Cockney figure so devoted to Crowmarsh, and bustling always so buoyantly, naïvely, and possessively about the outer fringe of his master's mysteries; and I was shown at once into Crowmarsh's room, where there was at present no sign of Crowmarsh.

A great deal has been written, and a great deal of nonsense has been talked, about Crowmarsh's methods and habits of life. A large portion of the public, in fact, still thinks of him as a sort of mad scientist in a childish German film, a creature garbed in something akin to a white Ku-Klux-Klan costume, surrounded by unholy retorts, crucibles, etc., and making mystic gestures and generating sparks and lightning from the abracadabraish machinery at his disposal. Anything less like the matter-of-fact Crowmarsh could, of course, not be imagined.

In fact, this tall, slightly sarcastic man always seemed to me to resemble a Harley Street specialist more than anything else, and all his surroundings and methods reinforced the notion of him as such. The room into which I was now shown was for all the world the image of any consulting-room of any well-to-do medical man – you felt three guineas out of pocket just to sit down in his arm-chair and look around. There was the large high window, the dingy outlook upon the brownish brick backs of other houses, the soft carpet, the mediocre pictures, the massive desk with telephone and engagement-book, the beautiful fountain-pen and the wonderful little chromium-plated calendar which you worked by twisting things at the side. There was even the silver-framed photograph of a pretty girl which you nearly always see in rooms of this kind, and which I always suspect is put there by its occupant to warn his women patients not to make love to him. This was the kind of room into which I was now put and left, and the crowning absurdity was reached when Fry, as an afterthought, came in and smilingly offered me a copy of *Punch* to read while I waited!

I was left waiting at least ten minutes, during which I heard vague noises and Crowmarsh's voice in the distance, and I need not describe my sensations during that time. You may think that this indifferent, matter-of-fact atmosphere should have calmed me down – indeed I told myself at the time that it had been engineered with that object in view: but actually it had the contrary effect, and by the time the immaculately-dressed Crowmarsh at last condescended to enter, I was so paralysed with fright and anguished expectancy I could barely open my mouth to greet him.

His manner of greeting me was of a piece with everything else – calm, matter-of-fact, almost distracted, as though I had come round to have a not particularly interesting photograph taken of my inside. I have said that at the time I thought that this atmosphere was deliberately engineered. I have since come to revise that view. This sheer cold disinterest, I now believe, was simply the man. He had made enough fuss of me when he wanted me for his own purpose: now I had agreed, and he had me at his mercy, he had no more interest in me than as some necessary part of his detestable machinery. But I was foolish enough at the time to mistake his inhumanity for a subtle form of manly humanity.

Almost immediately after he had smiled his rather mechanical smile and shaken hands with me, he sat down in his chair in front of his desk, and with a murmured 'Excuse me a moment, will you?' began to read an opened letter which lay on his desk. This he went through with the utmost calm and unconsciousness of my presence, turning it over in his hand when he had finished it, and re-reading certain portions . . .

'Well, well, well,' he said, in a sort of half-facetious, half-absentminded way, as he put the letter down (and I do not know to this day whether those three 'wells' alluded in a general way to the letter, or to the situation as regards me). 'Will you have a cigarette?'

And he slid the box along the desk in my direction with a large, firm gesture which was characteristic of him.

'Thanks,' I said, hardly able to pick a cigarette out, my hand and fingers trembled so. He slid a box of matches along with the same kind of gesture, and I lit up. Evidently he himself was not going to smoke. There was then an awkward silence, which he obviously found in no way awkward.

'Is everything ready?' I said, simply in order to say something.

'Yes. Everything's ready,' he said, with the same air of not having his attention fully focused upon me. 'Baldock'll be down in a moment.' And there was another long silence.

'Feeling nervous?' he said, smiling a little and revealing belated signs of a little fellow-feeling, for which I was disproportionately grateful.

'Yes. I am a bit.'

'Well, there's nothing to be nervous *about*,' he said in his slow voice. 'You know that, don't you?'

'Maybe. But I am. Wouldn't you be?'

'Oh – I don't know . . . ' he said, but got no further, for at this moment Roger Baldock entered.

There was an air of much greater sympathy and loquacious friendliness about this brilliant young assistant of Crowmarsh who has since become so famous. There was also an air, which he was unfortunately unable to conceal, of a young man engaged in one of the biggest larks of his life without any personal responsibility resting on his shoulders. In my terrified state I was much more sensitive to the latter aspect of his demeanour. Good God (I remember thinking), what are they going to do to me between them – this callous brute of a man and this inconsequent boy?

After three or four minutes' further conversation, which I cannot now remember anything about, Baldock produced a stethoscope from somewhere, and with a murmured 'This, of course, is just a formality' began to listen to my heart. He made no comment on what he heard, and put the instrument away. 'Well,' said Crowmarsh, 'let's go upstairs, shall we?'

And from this moment, I believe I can truthfully say that my sufferings ended, for I was no longer there to suffer. I was another, unlocated self, observing the three of us, hearing myself talking with the rest, noting every detail of our behaviour with disinterested gravity. I was aware even at the time that this feeling was none other than that merciful one so often spoken of by victims who have awaited judgment or execution. I can only describe it as a feeling of not *belonging* to my surroundings – of being therefore untouchable. If I had any fear now it was only the fear that this feeling would go.

Of what happened when we reached our destination – the most famous room in the world, on the third floor – I can now remember very little. I can remember Baldock disappearing, and Crowmarsh offering me another cigarette. I can remember taking about three puffs at this, and then putting it out. Then I can remember shaking hands with both of them, and walking, or rather climbing, into the *Asteradio* itself, without any sort of ado. A moment afterwards the door was closed.

There have been so many thousands of descriptions of the *Asteradio*, and so many photographs and drawings of it published in the Press, that it would be idle for me to add anything of that sort here. The superficial appearance of this extraordinary piece of mechanism – if 'mechanism' is a legitimate word – resembling, as it always does to me, a sort of mad cross between a telephone booth, a cabinet gramophone, an electric chair, a lift, a wardrobe mirror, an Iron Maiden and a huge camera – is as well known to any man in the street as it is by myself. The only thing, I believe, which nearly always impresses those who have actually beheld it, 'in the flesh', however, is the extraordinary air it has of crudity, of being a contraption, 'put together' in a haphazard way. I do not know what exactly it is that one finds lacking – something, I think, in greater dramatic accordance with its world-shaking potentialities, something more glittering, piercingly efficient and mysterious, something, in other words, more in the Mad Scientist tradition. What you actually see is something you feel your younger boy could have put together at home.

I am afraid, then, that those of my readers will be disappointed who had hoped that I might be able to throw any fresh light upon the invention itself. And here I should also make it clear that I am not in a position to make any contribution to any of those other controversies concerning time, dual presence, and identity which are raging around us now. I know the main question the layman wants to ask. Was my body, in the months in which I was millions of miles away in space, at one and the same time enclosed in the *Asteradio* machine on the third floor of Chandos Street? I cannot answer that question. Crowmarsh continually reiterates that that 'is not putting the question in the right way'. We are left in the dark, and sometimes forced to wish that he would be good enough to put the question in the 'right way' himself, and give us the right answer! But so far he has given no sign of doing that.

The point here is that I, having made by this machine the most momentous journey in the history of mankind, am as ignorant of the nature of my means of transport as any man in the street. I can only describe my sensations, and leave it at that.

Many people have asked me, not without a certain awed look on their faces, what my feelings were when the door was closed, and I knew the moment had come. I am afraid I am a disappointment even here as well, for that merciful feeling of numbness still persisted, and I had no sensations whatever – at least no sensations other than those of detached curiosity as to what was to befall that remote – that not totally credible figure – myself. As is known, the *Asteradio* is lit inside with what appears to be a common-or-garden electric bulb. I sat there, looking in turn at the five reflections of myself in the famous five steel mirrors which enclosed me all about. I remember remarking to myself what an ideal contraption this would be for a vain woman, and thinking that Crowmarsh at least should be able to sell his invention to the hairdressing profession if all else failed. Then I looked straight ahead at the reflection dead in front of me, and waited for the works to begin.

They were not tardy in giving me the works. I could just hear them moving about outside, and I sensed an air of bustle and excitement conspicuously lacking in their behaviour a few minutes ago. I heard Baldock give a sort of shout, and then there was a bang, and what I fancied was a curse, as though a table had been overturned accidentally. Finally there came a long droning sound, which was followed by the chug-chugging of what sounded more like the engine of a motor boat than anything else on earth. With this was combined an occasional rumbling noise, as of a distant sliding door.

I cannot possibly describe how incongruous and inadequate to the greatness and the seriousness of the occasion the next few minutes were. The chugging stopped – the droning began again – the droning stopped – the chugging began again – there was a pause in which nothing happened at all. I might have been in some third-rate Swiss train which for some reason could not get out of its station. Again I heard sounds of bustling and banging outside. I surmised that something had gone wrong, and that the whole thing was developing into a farce. Indeed I was just beginning to speculate as to whether I might cry out in question or protest to those outside, when I began to feel that something was happening.

I don't know how it was, but it seemed all at once as though the guard had blown his whistle. The droning sound began to coincide with the sound of the 'motor boat' and both increased in volume. The steel mirrors began to rattle, and I found that I was being gently shaken. Yet panic still was held at bay.

What things happened next to me, and the order in which they happened, are almost impossible to recapture, let alone to relate. I think the next thing I was aware of was the fact that the electric light within was burning with extraordinary, with ferocious, brightness, and at the same time I realized in a flash that I was intolerably hot and almost gasping for air. I looked in the mirror and saw the perspiration pouring down my face.

How had I got into this extraordinary condition? I looked as though I had been pouring sweat for hours. I was conscious of a wild singing noise in my ears, and felt like one in a delirious dream. Was I dreaming? Worse still (the thought suddenly struck me), had I *been* dreaming? Had I been *asleep?* A wave of uncontrollable fear and claustrophobia swept over me as it dawned upon me that this was precisely what had happened. I had been asleep – I had been incarcerated in this hellish contrivance for hours and hours! The horrible thing was that it was exactly six o'clock in the evening! I knew the hour in the world outside with a passionate lucidity and assurance which no man-made time-piece could have ever given me. Outside, all London was going home, taking trains, climbing on to buses ... And to me, only a moment ago, it had been ten o'clock in the morning!

I could not breathe, and I was going to die. Certainly I was going to die – the victim of a crude experiment. My heart could never withstand this heat and this noise – above all the noise – that was worse than the heat. There was a droning roar in my ears like that of twenty-thousand tube-trains crashing into tunnels ...

There had been some horrible accident or miscalculation on Crowmarsh's part, but how could I ever get out? Even if I yelled, how could I be heard now above this noise? Besides which, it paralysed my every faculty. I could not move a finger, an eyelid, let alone raise my voice.

I looked at myself again in the steel mirror, to see what manner of thing it was, this thing that had lived, and now was going to die. For a moment I saw my sodden and agonized face in that excruciating glare (the light itself seemed almost as heartbreaking as the noise and heat) – and then something else happened. I became aware that I was not looking at myself in the mirror. I occupied the space a moment ago occupied by the mirror, and I was looking at myself, noting every detail of my streaming face.

The relief was instantaneous and enormous. The noise, the light, the heat persisted – but some form of extemporized logic informed me that it was beyond their power to hurt the mere reflection of a man. I disowned that wretch sitting there fighting for breath. I wanted nothing but to go to sleep. I believe I went to sleep.

Whether I slept or not my next experience was one of floating in the infinite dark of an infinite void of noise. The noise for a moment had been dimmed, but now it was coming back – or rather it had been going on all the time, and now I was forced to hear it once more.

What followed I can never describe in words. To compare what I now experienced, with what I had experienced before I seemed to sleep, would be to compare the falling of a pin on a piece of cottonwool with the explosion of a munition works. It seemed that my being had become attuned to every sound that had been made, would be made, could be made by motion and power since time failed to begin! A man goes down to the engine-room of a ship and hears its driving-power throbbing through him. I was down in the engine-room of the Universe! Believe me, there is something of a roar down there.

I do not care to dwell upon what I suffered in the next few 'minutes' – for along with this terrible noise surging in upon me, there surged in upon me something worse – an even more horrible Knowledge! And the Knowledge was the Noise, and the Noise was the Knowledge – one and the same thing, and equally emphatic!

'*You're wrong! – you're wrong! – you're wrong!*' In some way my soul was screaming these words in the rhythm of what I was hearing. And another part of me was aware that I was addressing Abel Crowmarsh himself.

That Crowmarsh had made a ghastly mistake, a hideous miscalculation of realities – that he had, as a puny and ignorant mortal, intruded upon forces of inconceivable vastness and menace – this was the thought that obsessed me, which I felt I must somehow remember and take back with me, if ever I got back! No one must suffer again what I was suffering now. I knew all – he knew nothing.

And then somehow even this madly urgent truth seemed to be losing its significance – remained a truth, but was being submerged in another and even vaster truth.

'*It's two – it's two – it's two!*' I can remember screaming. And it was the Universe I was alluding to, and I had unravelled all its mysteries. But behind all mysteries, it seems, there is the mystery of oblivion, and oblivion came upon me then.

I need hardly say that Crowmarsh has since awarded not a jot of objectivity to these experiences of mine on my journey through the wastes of space, and has pointed out their similarity to countless other painful experiences undergone by people under common anaesthesia, which was a condition he actually predicted as being almost certainly attendant upon the undertaking. I myself have neither the requisite knowledge, nor the requisite inner conviction, to dispute the matter with him. Certainly (and here again I resemble innumerable other returned wanderers from the land of anaesthesia) I have no inkling now of that infinite 'Knowledge' which took the form of infinite sound, and which I was so desperately anxious to bring back with me to this world. As for that final cry and conviction of the 'twoness' implicit in all things, I really have no notion of what I meant. I have no doubt it is susceptible to hundreds of objective or subjective explanations – each equally satisfying to its propounder – the mystic, the brain-specialist, the heart-specialist, the nerve-specialist, the anaesthetist, even, it seems to me, the Hegelian or dialectical materialist! – but I myself am unable to contribute to the discussion.

As regards the pain, the sense of a mistake having been made, the terrible assurance I had that no man must again suffer what I had been set to suffer, well, I am not so sure of that now. How many women, in the pangs of childbirth, have not sworn to themselves that such an experience must never be renewed by themselves? We all know the fate of that determination – and am I not in like case? I can only tell you that I, for one, would make the journey again – will make it again, if I have the chance.

# CHAPTER TWO

Just as I have been asked by so many people what my feelings were when the door of the *Asteradio* was finally closed, and my journey lay ahead, so any number of others have wanted to know my first sensations on waking in Moribundia, and knowing that the farthest journey ever taken by man was at an end. Did I know where I was? – did I know who I was? – did I remember what had happened to me? – was I afraid? – and so on and so forth.

The answer is that I felt nothing more than the ordinary sensation of waking from sleeping – combined with the knowledge that I was rather cold, and that this in fact was what was waking me. I remembered what had happened to me, who I was, and what I was doing, with the utmost clarity and incisiveness. I was not afraid, but I wanted to do some more thinking before I opened my eyes and faced facts.

Above all I was filled with a profound sense of peace – the beautiful peace of victorious endeavour, and safety after peril. I wanted to go on lying where I was, draining this sense of peace to the dregs.

I suppose part of this feeling of comfort derived from the knowledge that I was in an atmosphere in which I could breathe and live, and the assurance, imbibed eagerly through every sense, that the scene to which I must at last open my eyes, was to bear countless features similar to those in the world from which I had come.

To begin with, I had put out my hand, and had made certain that I was lying upon grass – grass, moreover, which the sun had only left a little while ago. I myself was now in shadow, but I was certain the sun was still shining in the sky. It was either dawn or evening – I could not say which – the coolness, peacefulness, and freshness suggested either.

Still keeping my eyes closed, I began to listen intently for other sounds – but at first could pick up nothing – certainly no sound of anything like 'human' beings. I thought once that I could hear the sound of a fountain playing, but decided it was just a fuzziness in my own ears. At last, however, I became conscious of a very slight but recurring and curiously insistent sound.

I can only convey this sound (as it thus presented itself to my mind) by writing the word 'Pock.' It was a sound a man can make by placing his lips tightly together, and quickly snapping them open – a hollow sound you can sometimes hear in a slowly dripping tap. I could not make out whether it was very far away or very near, but finally I discerned that it possessed a definite periodicity of its own.

This curiously irritating little explosion came upon the ear about every fifteen seconds, but after every sixth explosion (as I judged) it ceased for nearly a minute, and then began again.

But sometimes there was a 'pock' or two missing in the series of six, and every now and again another sound intruded. This second sound was like the sound of dried peas being slowly turned over in a hollow cylindrical box – or of a gentle wave leaping from a soft sea on to a dreamy beach about a quarter of a mile away . . . But as this sound invariably succeeded, and seemed dependent upon, the 'pock' sound, I had to conclude that it came from no such romantic source. Occasionally, mingling with, or rising above this second sound, I thought I could hear the dim murmur and cry of distant human voices, but I presumed that this was my imagination.

I do not know how long I might have gone on listening to this sound – which had a lulling effect upon me in my peaceful state – had I not been visited with a sudden idea which made me jump.

Pock ... pock ... pock ... and then a sinister little rattle ... A *snake!* What else? And within a few inches of me! I swung up into an erect position, and opened my eyes.

I was on a green clipped lawn, surrounded on all sides by the sweet and venerable cloisters of what I immediately saw must be some cathedral or abbey. The gentle evening sun, lighting the green grass to flame at the farther end, shone athwart a scene as typically and gracefully English as anything English I had ever seen. There was no snake or crawling monster near me, and the thought of such a thing was preposterous.

Looking back at it now, I am astonished by the way, in the moments that followed, I took what I saw for granted – totally ignored the stupendous implications of that to which my eyes and senses bore testimony. That blind matter, developing into mind, acting upon itself, and growing self-conscious on a world other than ours, should have proceeded along paths of evolution so astonishingly similar, so that it finally culminated in such familiar phenomena as Gothic (yes, Gothic!) arches and clipped green lawns – here indeed was evidence of a new kind over which the mechanical materialist and the subjective idealist might continue their endless wrangle! But neither this thought – nor the thought of the fame I should win when I returned with this news to our world – even crossed my mind. I suppose I was in a sort of dream.

I stood still for a few minutes – merely gratefully accepting what I saw – and then, treading softly, made my way into the shade of the cloisters themselves.

My sole desire now was to locate the source of those gentle, but peculiarly exciting and perturbing little noises I had heard when my eyes were closed, and which still beat upon my ear. I walked down a dark avenue of arches, at the end of which I had espied, as at the end of a mighty telescope, a glimmering opening, and beyond that some trees.

I found my heart beating faster as I neared the end of this, and with something more than mere wonderment as to what I was going to see. I had a strange feeling that something was happening, that something of considerable moment was 'on,' only a matter of a few hundred yards away – something which would also account for the electric atmosphere, the breathless hush in which this venerable building and its environment seemed at the moment to be steeped.

I had no sooner emerged again into the light of day than a flash of inspiration seized me. About fifty yards ahead was a long row of trees planted closely together, and glimmering beyond them I had had a glimpse of white forms on a green background which made me quiver with expectation. A few seconds later my keenest hopes were confirmed, and everything which had puzzled me had been clarified.

The white forms were the forms of boys in flannels, and the 'pocking' sound which, with my eyes closed, I had nervously mistaken for the advance of a reptile, was no other sound than that sweetest of all sweet and nostalgic sounds to the breast of every Englishman, the sound of bat upon ball! And the sound of the peas in the cylindrical box, of the soft wave on the nearby beach, came from nothing but the little swelling bursts of applause – the intermittent clapping of the spectators who were in the pavilion, or lying on the grass around!

I realized instantly that, as might have been expected, there was a public-school attached to the religious building from which

I had emerged, and that the whole life of its young and grown-up inhabitants was at present absorbed by, fiercely concentrated upon, the cricket match in progress – which was no doubt a serious event against a visiting school. No wonder I had had that feeling of tension.

The pavilion, packed as I could see from here, with a crowd of relations and masters, was at the far end of the ground from where I stood, and all around, seated on benches or lying sprawled on the ground, were the boys – every member of this far-flung circle of young and old gazing at the centre of the field with the immobility of Red Indians in ambush.

It was, indeed, as though this, the very first of the strange scenes I was to witness in the land of Moribundia, had been specially prepared for me – so arranged that the members of the community were spread out before me, for my benefit, as it were, in a state of absolute naturalness and unself-consciousness, and so absorbed in their own rites that a stranger could move among them with less conspicuousness than a ghost.

I knew at once that I must seize this moment – drink in these unspoiled impressions while I could, and keeping close to the trees, I began to circle slowly but without stealth in the direction of the pavilion.

It was not until I had passed the second or third group of boys lying sprawled upon the grass that I became aware that something was 'wrong' – had my first intimation, in other words, that this world into which I had come had certain physical characteristics and peculiarities which differed, however faintly, from those in the world from which I had come. There was, in fact, something 'wrong' about these boys themselves. And this something 'wrong' derived from the fact that there was something much too 'right' about them.

To one accustomed to the lean, lanky, pimpled, and somewhat smutty appearance of the average public-school boy in England, there was an air of sunburned masculinity about each of these boys I was now looking at – of handsome muscular earnestness, of lissom gracefulness, of blue-eyed burning idealism, of manly fortitude, of disciplined (above all, disciplined) perfection, which simply took one's breath away. Gazing intently at the game, with their eager profiles presented to me, they seemed a set of young dreaming Raleighs. And indeed, it was clear enough that, in looking at the game, they were seeing something more than a mere game – they were looking into their own future, imbibing lessons of sportsmanship, self-sacrifice, and courage which would certainly serve them in good stead in the battle of life ahead.

A thrill ran through me as it occurred to me that I had, perhaps, alighted upon a world of ideal creatures, of gods – or demi-gods at last. I did not know then what I found out later, that in Moribundia this perfection of spiritual and physical demeanour was confined exclusively to public-school boys or ex-public-school boys – to a race, or caste, known in a general way as the *Akkup Bihas* – and that each other caste, without necessarily being considered lower in grade, had a completely different set of characteristics, sometimes very much the opposite of perfect, and exaggerated upon lines of its own.

As I drew nearer to the pavilion I began to look at the adults, who were either seated on the benches, or standing in little groups around. I did not care to get too close to them, but I was at once struck by the immaculateness of their clothes and their figures – all of which (those of the women and men alike) were tall and willowy, to a remarkable, almost fantastic degree. That this was a fixed peculiarity of the adult *Akkup Bihas*, by which he might be instantly recognized from a good distance off, I did not of course then know – any more than I knew that there was another class, the *Gnikrow* class, which was characterized by a somewhat detestable shortness and round-shouldered squatness. This well-defined physical distinction between classes, and even professions, was one of the features of Moribundia which made things very simple in some respects for the newcomer. For instance, whereas an unpleasantly corpulent member of the class of the *Akkup Bihas* was a thing practically inconceivable in this strange land, the idea of a thin *Reknab*, or a thin *Rekamkoob*, or a thin *Reetiforp*, was equally out of the question.

But I am anticipating. Choosing a spot on the grass as near to the pavilion as I dared, I sat down and began to look at the game itself. It was at once evident that the tenseness and quietness, the breathless hush prevailing everywhere, was due to the fact that a climactic and crucial moment had been reached. The scoreboard showed that the other side had totalled 120, and that the side now batting had produced 111 runs for 8 wickets. Ten more runs to make and two wickets to fall! – in schoolboy cricket about as thrilling a situation as you could desire.

For the next five minutes or so I watched the game with rapt attention. In three overs no further run was scored, and yet the pair at the wicket seemed to be holding their own. This in itself (although I know very little about cricket) seemed to me something of a feat, as the pitch was bumping fiercely, and the light of the declining sun had a blinding quality which I should imagine must have made the ball very hard to see.

Hearing a noise behind me, I turned my head and saw near to me a boy of from twelve to fourteen years of age, wearing white flannels and putting on cricket-pads. It was at once evident to me that he was the last man in, and that when the next wicket fell the game would depend upon him.

As I looked at this boy, admiring his extreme good looks, and the calm, determined expression on his face, I saw, approaching him from behind, another boy, older, taller and of an even more noble appearance.

There followed a curious incident. The older boy, coming up unnoticed from behind until he was within close range, suddenly raised his hand and smote the other on the shoulders with a smack so violent and resounding that I half expected to see its recipient fall to the ground.

Instead of this, however, and instead of resenting this assault from the back in any way, the younger boy turned, with that peculiar upright grace of manner which showed in every movement made by these young super-men, and faced his Captain (for the Captain of the team it obviously was) with a look of disciplined expectancy and manly adoration astonishing in its intensity.

What followed was even more curious still. For a moment or two there was a silence in which they glared, half-hypnotically, into each other's eyes. Then the Captain spoke.

'Play up,' he said, in a ringing, measured, almost savagely emphatic tone. 'Play up! – and *play the game!*'

He then walked immediately away with the slightly jaunty air of a man by no means displeased at having been able to express his requirements in so precise a manner.

I must confess that this little episode, which, I was soon to learn, was entirely in keeping with the whole strange atmosphere and standards of behaviour of Moribundia, filled me at the time with something like apprehension. I began to suspect, in fact, that I was in the society of people not very far removed from lunatics. However, my attention was diverted at that moment by a kind of whoop and murmur all around the ground, and looking out again at the field I saw that another wicket had fallen – the ninth. Now, indeed, it was up to the last man if the game was to be saved!

Full of excitement myself, I looked eagerly at the face of the boy whose shoulder had been hit so hard, and upon whom so much now depended. I can truthfully say that I have never seen such a wonderful expression on any boy's face. It amazed me that a mere game, a mere school cricket match, could evoke so brave and lovely a gleam of selflessness and determination. I stress the selflessness, for it was obviously not for the thought of any fame he might win that season amongst his school-fellows, nor was it for any hope of getting a permanent place in the first eleven and so having the privilege of wearing a blazer (a curious ribboned affair – rather exotic, I thought) like his Captain's – that this boy meant to go in and win. No, it was because his Captain had hit him upon the shoulder and told him to play up, and to play the game.

At that moment of impact, so strong had been the hypnotic force which I had felt flowing from the Captain, through the Captain's hand, into the boy's shoulder, and so on into the boy, that to me it was an almost foregone conclusion that he would succeed now in making the ten runs required. And I was proved right. After leaving two balls on the off-side severely alone, he hit a four off the last ball of the over; there was a tense maiden over at the other end; and then, having played forward to two balls cautiously and with a very straight bat (I noticed, by the way, that these youngsters had been taught to hold their bats and play every stroke with a positively Prussian straightness which I could not help feeling was in some measure cramping their style), our friend hit a glorious six clean over the pavilion, the heads of the parents and the masters, and the game was over.

A storm of applause and cheering broke out on all sides, the players came in, and a thing happened which I have never actually seen happen in any English public-school, or in any school at all for that matter – the boy, now the hero of the match, was lifted high upon the shoulders of his friends, and amidst shouts and cheers and the singing of 'For he's a jolly good fellow' carried back in triumph all the way to the school buildings.

In concluding this chapter, this narration of my first adventure, if so it may be called, in a new world, I cannot resist the temptation to say something about a remarkable poem which – after I had been some months in Moribundia and had settled down to a study of its literature – I came across quite by accident in a popular anthology out there (or should I say *up* there?) bearing the title of *Smeop Fo Yadot*.

This poem was by one of Moribundia's most famous and most dearly cherished authors, *Yrneh Tlobwen*, but the effect it had upon me was caused not so much by its authorship or merits, as by the chord of memory it suddenly and almost alarmingly struck in me as I read it. The whole cricket match, and the whole scene, was described in this poem almost exactly as I had seen it. The breathless hush overhanging the Close, the bumping quality of the pitch, the blinding light, the state of the game, the amount of runs to be made, even the strange ribboned coat which the Captain wore, and the Captain's thunderous exhortation to his junior – all were set out within the limited space of the first verse!

My surprise at reading this can be imagined – as, for a moment or two, I felt certain that the author himself must actually have been present at this very cricket match I have been describing, must indeed have been standing within a few yards of where I had been standing, and have seen and felt what had been seen and felt by myself.

My feeling of wonderment, however, only lasted a few seconds.

As soon as I had had time to reflect I realized there was no coincidence in the matter at all. For I knew, by that time, that that thrilling sort of encounter, in which, at the end, there are ten runs to make and only one wicket to fall, was as common and ordinary event in Moribundia as any of those miserably dull affairs in England, in which, at the end, there are probably less than ten runs to make and ten wickets to fall.

I knew, in fact, that all those things which are dreamed about and fondly nurtured in the mind of the ordinary person on our own earth, were in the wonderful world of Moribundia transformed into hard truths, matters of concrete fact. I knew that that delightful scene of youthful idealism and sportsmanship which I had witnessed on the evening of my arrival was one which took place, in an almost identical form, wherever cricket matches were ever played by Moribundian schoolboys. In other words, I had by that time gleaned the inner secret of Moribundia – the land in which the ideals and ideas of our world, the striving and subconscious wishes of our time, the fictions and figments of our imagination, are calm, cold actualities. But I am still anticipating.

# CHAPTER THREE

I had been so absorbed in watching the emotional boys departing in that strange way, that I had not noticed that cars were being drawn up and were droning away from a spot behind the pavilion, and that amidst a general hubbub the parents were going off as well.

Consequently, I suddenly, as it were, woke up, to find myself alone in a silent, deserted playing field – a green, melancholy arena, recently so gay and full of life, but now filled with the bewildered sadness of a thing from which something has been suddenly and unreasonably snatched away, so that it seemed to look as your friend might look, if, at a moment when the conversation was at its brightest and most confidential, you had struck him in the face and walked away. Denuded even of the cricket stumps, stuck proudly in its middle a few minutes ago, it seemed to be wondering 'what it had done'.

At another time I might have extracted some aesthetic enjoyment from this scene: in my present circumstances, it had the contrary effect: a sudden realization of my precarious and uncanny situation in this world, my isolation, the vast distance (vaster than any man had ever known) dividing me from my friends and familiar things, flooded in upon me, and I was filled with loneliness and fright.

What was I to do now? Where was I to go? What was the rest of this world like? To whom was I to speak? Was it safe to speak to anyone? Would the people be friendly? How conspicuous would I be? How was I to live – to keep body and bone together – if I did not make myself known? Could I even make myself understood? I was lost – marooned! I cursed myself for a fool for being so utterly mentally unprepared for the difficulties and perils which anyone in their senses would have realized must beset a man coming out of the blue into a new world. I cursed Crowmarsh for his damned inconsequence. I even thought ill of my best friends, who had thought so little about the matter, and who had said good-bye to me with the same sort of cheerful complacency one shows in seeing an acquaintance off in a train for a week-end at Margate.

Suddenly a thought struck me which reassured me somewhat. Those words of the Captain – 'Play up – play up, and play the game' – had I not understood them as soon as they were uttered? In that case, had I not proof that the Moribundians spoke my own language – a language intelligible to myself. I cast my mind back, and tried to hear again what I had heard. No, the actual words spoken had fallen strangely upon my ears, had been uttered in a language I did not know – had sounded to me, now I thought about them, extraordinarily like Scandinavian, or Dutch (or double-Dutch, if you like!) – and yet I had been able to grasp their significance – their literal significance – without the slightest effort and at the moment they entered my ears and fell upon the brain within.

I should say now that this was one of the greatest mysteries of my extraordinary sojourn in this land. I never had, from the first moment, the slightest difficulty in understanding what was being said to me or all around me – and yet I never consciously made the smallest attempt to study the language or vocabulary. I can make no attempt to explain this satisfactorily: I can only say that I had a feeling while I was there, a very definite feeling, that my mind had been in some way reset, turned round, *readjusted*; so that the

Moribundian language – whose diction will seem so harsh and whose general appearance will seem so unfamiliar to an English reader – was to me lucid, elegant, and simple – while, for the time being, my own language seemed uncouth and strange, so that I did not care to think in it or about it. I can only presume that the gift temporarily awarded to me was akin to that said to be possessed by mediums and others who, we are led to understand, often know five or six languages which they obviously do not know. To me there does not seem anything specially remarkable in such a thing happening to me – if you are a Crowmarsh and choose to spend your days sedulously playing ball with (and I might say, occasionally tweaking the noses of) such odd and dangerous gentlemen as Father Time and Uncle Space, you can hardly complain when something oddly resembling a supernatural miracle turns up every now and again.

But I am again out of my depth. No such reflections entered my head as I realized that I was going to understand and be understood in this new world. I merely felt a certain relief, and was encouraged to look around me, and set about making some plans.

First of all, *where* was I? If this school corresponded to the average public-school in England, presumably I was in the depths of the country somewhere. Was that good or bad? Should I, to begin with, hide in the country, or should I somehow make my way to a big town? A little reflection decided me in favour of the latter. In a large town I would be less conspicuous; and also I had at the back of my mind the idea of finding, perhaps, some central cultural or scientific institution, whose officials might find my story credible. But that would only be a last resort. Anything in the nature of a formal welcome, with the vast publicity it would entail, was what I most wanted to avoid. Such a thing might come later, and very pleasant and comfortable it might be, but so long as it could possibly be continued, my duty to science lay in observing this world and these people while they were not observing me, in studying their life, not in the selected, unreal and self-conscious form in which a modern royalty in our own world is compelled to see it, but as it was lived, by simple people, without a trace of self-consciousness, from day to day.

I was now walking under some trees, beyond which I had discerned a low wall, on the other side of which I suspected there was a more or less deserted country road. All at once I stopped, listening to an approaching sound which fell familiarly on my ears – the sound, it seemed to me, of a motor bus.

I had not to wait long. It was a motor bus all right, and in a few seconds I saw its red-enamel exterior flashing through the green of the trees. It was going at a good speed along the road the other side of the wall, and in a few more seconds its uproar had diminished again, and it had vanished. But a sight and sound again so familiar had left my heart lighter.

I had noticed, also, that it was a double-decker, with an open top – nothing in the nature of a 'char-a-banc', or 'motor coach'. From this I thought it justifiable to conclude that this place could not be very far from a fair-sized town, and I had already half-decided to jump on to the next bus that came along.

I reached the wall, climbed over it without difficulty, and found myself on the road. To my right this stretched away into practically unspoiled country scenery, to my left it led down a hill to what I took to be a village of some sort. And in the distance beyond the village I could see all the evidences of a straggling urban population. It looked like the beginnings of a great town, and of course it was – since *Tlobwen Yebba*, on whose site the school is built, is in point of fact only ten miles from the centre of *Nwotsemaht* itself, bearing the same sort of geographical relation to this, the capital and centre of Moribundia, as, let us say, Harrow bears to our own metropolis.

I walked in a sort of dream down towards the village, and if I encountered anyone on the way I do not remember it. Nor am I able to remember the faces or appearances of anyone I saw when I got there, though I must have passed at least a dozen people. This may seem absurd, but I suppose my still bewildered thoughts were somehow occupied elsewhere, drinking in other impressions. In fact, I can remember very little about the village itself, except that it was aesthetically disappointing, any sign of antiquity it may once have displayed being completely shoved out of the way by ugly shop-fronts of recent date and by the exigencies of the motor car – petrol stations, hoardings, signs, cement roads, and, in what I took to be its centre, a 'roundabout' in place of what may have once been a market-place.

It was on the other side of this 'roundabout' that I saw all that interested me at the moment – a sign on a lamp-post saying 'Buses Stop Here'. And on a framed sign underneath this was written: 'Service to *Nwotsemaht*', and a list of times and stopping places. These meant very little to me, as the ticking of my watch had not survived a journey by *Asteradio* (the feeble little hands pointed still to a quarter past ten of a Chandos Street morning!), and I did not yet know what the names of the places might signify. I judged, however, by the light in the sky, that in Moribundia it must be about a quarter-past five of a summer's afternoon. The question as to what time it now was in our own world, or indeed what remote era in the past or future of our world, I leave to Crowmarsh and his friends.

I was able to observe, too, that the service was a very frequent one, and almost before I was ready for it – that is, before I had fully made up my mind that the best course open to me was to take a bus into the town, another bus came along.

At the same moment two other people who had apparently been waiting for the same bus, appeared, seemingly from nowhere, as they do on these occasions, and one of them politely stood aside to let me get on first. As I was fearful of making myself in any way conspicuous, my mind was made up for me, and I quickly mounted the step. I took a seat inside and the bus restarted.

# CHAPTER FOUR

Still afraid that in some way my appearance must be incongruous and likely to give me away, I did not have the courage to look at my travelling companions for the first few minutes (though I was aware that the bus was about a quarter full), and instead averted my face by looking out of the window.

We were soon in the midst of narrow streets with buildings and shops each side, and there was no more doubt in my mind that the country had been left behind for good, and that we were heading for the centre of the metropolis, however distant that might be.

I may say that I saw enough in the streets, even in those few minutes looking out of the window, to fill me with the greatest interest, and every kind of surmise and bewilderment, but I shall be describing the streets, and the Moribundian scene generally, later. My attention was soon diverted, in any case, by some decidedly droll sounds coming from the top of the bus – the sound of heavy feet stamping about on the wooden floor, and a voice raised in tones of the extremest joviality.

My first impression was that there must be a drunken man up there, and I stole a furtive glance at my neighbours to see if they were hearing what I was hearing and showing any signs of alarm or amusement. They, however (quite an ordinary bunch of people, such as you might see in any bus in England), sat stolidly in their seats and did not seem to be aware of anything out of the ordinary taking place. As the noise upstairs seemed to be growing louder and louder, this struck me as very strange.

I next looked round for the conductor, to see whether he was doing anything about it. But there was no conductor present. Was he upstairs, trying to persuade the drunkard to get off the bus?

Imagine my surprise when, a few moments later, I heard the same heavy footsteps, carrying the owner of the same jovial voice, coming down the steps of the bus, and I realized that these raucous good spirits, which I had presumed to be those of a drunken man, proceeded from the conductor himself!

I do not know how I am going to convey to the reader the overwhelming personality of this bus-conductor, nor the effect he had upon me, but as he resembled, in almost every particular, every bus-conductor I met in Moribundia (and every bus-draw; and taxi-driver, and engine-driver, too, if it comes to that), I must certainly make the attempt.

To tell my present reader that he was the living image of the greater part of the drawings of a well-known Moribundian black-and-white artist – one *Treb Samoht* – and also those of another artist, *Ecurb Rehtafsnriab* – will, of course, be to tell him nothing. He has never seen the work of these artists, and unless he makes the same journey that I made, he never will. All the same, I only wish that I could have brought some specimens home with me, for the written word is powerless to depict adequately the grotesque appearance, yet stupendous demeanour, of those engaged to manage public vehicles in Moribundia.

I can speak of corpulence, and I can speak of joviality: I can speak of red noses, and I can speak of enormous moustaches. But how am I going to make credible or real, to anyone in our workaday world, the seven-chinned fatness of face, the wild and rolling obesity, of the man I now saw – the glorious heartiness, as of a dozen Cheeryble brothers rolled into one, of his manner; the raw, flaming redness of his enlarged nose (I actually fancied

I could perceive rays bursting from it which lit the air around it), or the tempestuous cascade which was his moustache!

As, with an outward appearance such as his, no sort of behaviour in which he could indulge could really be regarded as strange, I realized at once that he was not drunk, though it would have been fairly obvious to a medical man that he was not averse to the bottle in his hours off duty. But as soon as I began to listen to his speech, and I may say he hardly ever left off talking, I had further cause for wonderment.

I should say that his language was quite as grotesque as his appearance, if not more so. Characterized, as it was, by incessant, deliberate, and, as it were, vindictive distortions and vulgarizations of the language and its correct accent, I had never heard the like of it. The fact that, in the town of *Nwotsemaht*, *all* bus-conductors, all bus-drivers, all taxi-drivers, all engine-drivers, in fact all those employed in the more menial side of transport, talked in the same way, I did not then know. Nor did I know that it was a recognized thing – that such workers were, by the ordinance of some rigid Moribundian law, chosen only from the ranks of a class of beings known as *Yenkcocs*, who could think and enunciate in this way and in no other. Eventually I got hardened to it, but to one used to the smooth, quiet, reasonable accent of an average London bus-conductor (possibly a little coloured by the locality in which he has been born, but nothing more), it was at first positively agonizing to hear.

As this Moribundian *Yenkcoc* language is like nothing that has ever been heard on earth, just as the exterior of the *Yenkcoc* bus-conductor was like nothing that has ever been seen on earth, it is not easy for me to give a satisfactory impression of it here.

If I gave a list of the obscure and extraordinary expressions – such as: 'Blimey', 'Crikey', 'Cripes', 'Bloomin'', 'Blinkin'', 'Ruddy', 'S'welp-me', 'Coo', 'Struth', 'Strike me pink', 'Yerdontsay', 'Gawd', 'Lorblessyer', 'Lorluverduck', 'Arfamo', 'Lumme', etc. – without uttering one, or several of which expressions, the Moribundian *Yenkcoc* is hardly able to utter a sentence – I might go on for ever. But these expressions play only a minor role in the hideousness and uncouthness of the general effect – which is obtained for the most part by wilful, you might say fervent, misplacing of aspirates, and the equally impassioned substitution of a wrong vowel-sound for the correct one whenever possible. However, I will continue my narrative, and the reader will be able to judge for himself.

It so happened that shortly after the conductor's coming inside to collect the fares, the driver, who had, so I thought, been driving very fast, was forced suddenly to swerve in order to avoid a cart. Although there was no damage done an old lady sitting opposite me (who belonged to a short-sighted, school-mistressy, prim, fussy type, of which I later saw a good deal in Moribundia, and learned to identify as the *Retsnips* type) was considerably shaken in her seat, and she ventured to say to the conductor that she thought the driver was going too fast.

'Horlright! Horlright! hold gal!' said, or rather yelled, this extraordinary conductor. 'Keep yer 'air on! Keep yer 'air on! That is,' he added, so that everybody could hear, but giving the old lady a salacious and knowing wink the like of which I had never seen, 'that is, if it *is* yer 'air, lidy, an' haint not nobody helses!'

And at this he went off into fits of the wildest laughter, which shook his whole body as it might have been shaken by an electrical machine. When he had recovered from this he spoke again.

'Looks like my mate,' he said, beaming all over, 'wants to get back to 'is missiz!' And at this he went to one of the windows, thrust his head out in the most inconsequent way, and hailed the driver.

'*Wotcher*, Alf!' he cried, to gain his attention.

'*Wotcher*, Bert!' cried the driver to signify he had heard.

I have here to confess that I have not the slightest idea of the meaning of this expression 'Wotcher' – but no *Yenkcoc* in Moribundia ever greets a friend, when he is any distance away from him, without making use of it. I may also fittingly remark, at this point, that in obedience to some caste tradition, which I do not understand, the only Christian names which the parents of *Yenkcocs* are able to bestow upon their male children, are 'Bert', 'Alf', 'Bill' or 'Fred'. 'Fred', actually, is rare. The surname of the Moribundian *Yenkcoc* is almost equally restricted: if he is not called Muggins he is called Juggins, and if he is not called Juggins he is called Buggins, and if he is not called Buggins he is called Sproggins. Again, you might occasionally come across a rarer form, such as Higgins (or Wiggins), but the termination 'gins' is rigidly adhered to, and it is never preceded by more than one syllable.

'Curb that there blinkin' himpetuous temperryment o' yourn, mate!' the conductor now yelled to the driver. 'There's an ole gal in 'ere wot's gettin' 'er false teeth rattled!'

'Horlright! Horlright!' yelled back the driver, whom I could see through the glass at the front, and whose corpulence, geniality, and liberality of moustache were on an even larger scale than that attained by his friend (while his bulbous nose burned with so fierce a ray, that, for an area of an inch or so around it, it definitely set up a sort of glaring white light which prevented me from seeing the scenery beyond it). 'Horlways willin' to hoblige a young leddy, lorblessyer!'

I do not know what the reader will have made of this dialogue up to now, or whether he will have felt in any degree what I felt very strongly at the time – surprise, not unmixed with chivalrous resentment, at what appeared to be gratuitous insolence brought to bear against a defenceless middle-aged lady. She had, in fact, been insulted outright four times in succession. She had first of all been told 'to keep her hair on', which implied that she was in such an absurd state of excitement that it might fly off. It had then been suggested that it was not really her hair at all – that she was wearing a wig. After that, it had been definitely stated that her teeth were false (which no doubt they were, but there was no need to call attention to the matter). Finally the driver had called her a 'young lady' in a sarcastic manner deliberately adopted to make clear the fact that she was no longer young.

It was on the tip of my tongue, in fact, to call these men to order. But I desisted for two reasons. Firstly, as I explained before, I dreaded making myself conspicuous. Secondly, I saw that the faces of those around me, so far from reflecting the resentment and anger rising in my own breast, bore instead a look of complacent approbation (not unmixed, perhaps, with a faintly bored look, as of people who had witnessed the same sort of scene many times before) which was very difficult to understand.

It was fortunate enough, as it happened, that I did desist from making any protest, as I do not know what might have happened to me had I done otherwise – something, possibly, very serious indeed.

The fact is that this sort of behaviour on the part of this class of person is, in Moribundia, looked upon with the greatest possible favour. Indeed, known as *Yenkcoc Ruomuh* – which means, roughly translated, 'the high spirits of the *Nwotsemaht* labouring man' – it is regarded with semi-religious respect. To deride, to criticize, or to doubt the existence of what is called *eht Gniliafnu Doog Ruomuh fo eht Gnikrow Sessalc* ('the incessantly gay temperament of the lower orders') is to call into question something which Moribundia holds dearest to its heart; and anyone so foolish, or, as I nearly was, so ignorant as to do so, might easily incur danger to his life. For Moribundians are in certain respects ruthless, as we shall see.

This may seem fantastic to people of our world – I mean to pay such profound, almost fetishistic homage to a type represented by this absurd bus-conductor – but I am not so sure that it is so. It must be remembered that this class is unlike anything we know in England. To make any comparison between the stupendous creature I have just described and the thin, quiet, sallow-faced, usually slightly dyspeptic and surly person in blue we encounter in an average London bus, would be quite absurd. Moribundia realizes, quite reasonably, I think, that this class, with its peculiar temperament, forms one of the most precious elements of its general well-being. For without these high spirits, this incessant and illogical cheerfulness, this delicious gaiety under irksome and difficult tasks, this taking of everything as a *joke*, it is doubtful whether any of the vaster Moribundian undertakings – such as, for instance, protracted wars (in which, alas, Moribundians are still, against all their dearest wishes and instincts, compelled to engage) – could be undertaken at all. Moribundia appreciates the fact, knows, if you like, which side its bread is buttered. And if, in this magnificent realization of the magnificent ideal of contentment, of constant day-to-day humour, the poor uneducated fellows occasionally take a liberty with their superiors, it is cheerfully and gratefully overlooked, if not definitely loved for its own sake. I may be wrong, but I should personally like to see Moribundian conductors on our own buses.

However, my view was not adjusted at that time, and my surprises had only just begun.

The conductor was now standing over the middle-aged lady, waiting to take her fare. This was a long time coming, as she did nothing but fumble in the depths of her bag, and seemed quite unable to produce the coin she wanted. At the same time she muttered irritably and fussily to herself, and nodded her head in a silly way.

The truth was that I was beginning to lose my sympathy for this lady. Of course, had I known that, in acting thus, she was merely making manifest the unalterable characteristics of every member of the *Retsnips* class, I might have made some allowance for her. As it was, her extreme plainness filled me with gloom, and her manners irritated me more and more.

She did eventually produce a coin – a florin. (The coinage of Moribundia so closely resembles our own that I can speak of florins, half-crowns, sixpences, etc.) Now as she was only taking a short journey, for which the fare was only one penny, this florin was, of course, far in excess of the fare, and it was necessary for the conductor to give her a lot of change. As this was inconvenient for him, she had the grace to apologize to him.

'I'm sorry,' she said, 'that I haven't a copper, conductor.'

'Bless yer 'art, lidy – don't take hon so!' replied the conductor, at the same time cautiously biting the coin to see that it was a genuine one. 'You're goaner 'ave twenty-three in arfamo!'

Now this reply (though undeniably rather rude) struck me as being extraordinarily witty, and I nearly burst out laughing. But the others, accustomed from childhood, as I now know, to the resource and sparkle of *Yenkcoc Ruomuh*, seemed to think nothing of it. Also, to tell the truth, they seemed to me to have the expression of people who have heard 'this one' more times than they cared to remember.

As I watched the conductor slowly and solemnly counting out the twenty-three coins into the wretched woman's hand, it suddenly occurred to me that it was my turn next – that I had to pay my fare! Why had I not thought of this, and what was I going to do? Where did I want to go in any case? While my thoughts were still in a semi-paralysed state, the conductor finished with his other customer, and stood in front of me, waiting for my money.

'Er—' I muttered, in a bewildered way. 'Do you – er – want the money for my fare?'

'Crikey, no, gent! Nothin' like *thet!*' said the conductor. 'Me an' Bert's just come aht fer a ruddy joy-ride! Ain't we, Bert?' he shouted out of the window.

'Gorblimey – yus! Course we 'ave, Alf,' shouted back the driver. 'Just to look at the bloomin', blinkin', blanketty-blank scenery – wot?'

While the two men continued to make fun of me in this droll manner, I dived in desperation into my pocket, and produced a sixpence. Mistaking this for a Moribundian piece, as anyone might have done, the conductor gave me a ticket in exchange for it, and no change. It was a great piece of good fortune that he thus absent-mindedly presumed that this was the ticket I was wanting. Had there been any further discussion I should probably have been discovered then and there. During all my stay in Moribundia I was never so near being found out as I was at that moment.

In the next three or four minutes, nothing, I think, of particular interest occurred. The bus, somewhat erratically and furiously driven, I noticed, forged ahead into streets growing more thickly populated every moment, and the stopping places grew more and more frequent.

At one of these stopping places two people got off, and three more got on. The first of these was a girl, so gloriously slim, clear-skinned and pretty that she took my breath away; the next was a big, dark, aggressive-looking man with a long nose and black tortoise-shell spectacles of a thickness and magnitude such as I have never seen on earth; the last was a gentleman whose face was swathed round and round with what I took to be flannel, and from whose right cheek there protruded the most horrible bulge. I was horrified at his appearance at the time, but later found out that the disease from which he was suffering was nothing graver than common toothache. In Moribundia toothache invariably takes this violent form – a state which has also been frequently depicted by such artists as *Samoht* and *Rehtafsnriab*. It is perhaps due to the Moribundians' nervous dread of going to their dentists, outside whose houses they will often walk about for hours on end, before summoning up the courage to go in.

As the beautiful girl sat down, she happened to cross her legs in order to get into a more comfortable position, and in so doing lifted her skirt almost to the level of her knee. If only you could have seen the look which came across the *Retsnips*' face at this! – the horror, the stiffening, the upturned nose, the sour-visaged and Puritanical disapproval! But it was clear to anyone that, thwarted in her own life, she was bitterly jealous of the other's good looks and youth.

As soon as the aggressive-looking man in the tortoise-shell spectacles had settled in his seat, he began to look around him, and talk at random to anyone who cared to listen. He had the most harsh, grating, nasal voice, and such a boastful, arrogant air that I at once took a dislike to him. The other people in the bus liked him no better, but seemed to take him very much for granted. Actually, there are hundreds upon hundreds of these vain, boastful people, roaming about all over Moribundia and making themselves offensive – particularly in the summer months and amidst scenes of old-world dignity. They are known as *Snacirema*. Their speech, again like nothing I have ever heard on earth, is indescribably hideous and difficult to render, but I must make the best attempt I can.

'Say, Bo,' he said sneeringly, looking round to criticize something the moment he had sat down, and lighting a huge cigar, or cheroot, the fumes of which nearly choked us all. 'Whaddya call this lil' tin can – an automobeel?'

'Yus, mate – wot's the matter with it?' said the conductor, for the moment nonplussed.

'Waal, Bo,' replied the *Nacirema*, 'I jes kinda guess we got real buses back in my countree. Yes, sir! Yep!' And at this he spat upon the floor.

The conductor was quick to recover himself.

'Well, chum,' he said. 'Wot you want fer a penny? A blinkin' private suite, wiv bathroom attached?'

Everybody laughed at this, and it was felt that the man had been effectually and deservedly snubbed.

He, however, seemed to have the hide of a rhinoceros so far as jokes against himself were concerned, and spat again upon the floor with the utmost composure.

At this moment the bus began to go at an alarming rate and to take corners in a most dangerous manner. This was naturally alarming to all of us, but particularly to the *Retsnips* sitting opposite, who began to show the liveliest signs of nervousness. At last she could bear it no longer.

'Oh, dear – oh, dear!' she cried. 'I'd give ten pounds to be out of this!'

'Don't waste your money, lidy,' shouted the conductor, amidst all the roar and lurching of the vehicle. 'You'll be out soon enough!'

This, of course, was anything but consoling to the lady – charming specimen of *Yenkcoc Ruomuh* as it was. And, frankly, I was now terrified. I had yet to acquire a knowledge of that absolute disregard of danger, and complete inconsequence with respect to serious accidents, which characterizes the Moribundian *Yenkcoc*. A good enough example of it was given me in the next minute. For, in taking a corner at a most reckless speed, the bus ran clean into a hand-driven cart piled high with fruit and vegetables. The owner of the cart, from his appearance obviously a *Yenkcoc* like the driver and conductor, was thrown up into the air, and landed in the gutter. All the fruit, of course, was also projected violently into the air, and fell, like a shower of hail, upon the owner. By a comic freak of chance, a single apple fell into his outstretched hand, and now, scratching his head with one hand, and holding the apple in the other, he looked at the apple in a whimsical way which was most amusing to see. The bus had stopped, with a great screaming of brakes, and I waited eagerly to see what was going to happen next.

The owner of the cart remained in this foolish position for nearly a quarter of a minute, and then, with the utmost good humour, and looking from the apple to the conductor and back again, spoke.

'Thanks, chum,' he said. 'Just the one I was wanting!'

Everybody laughed at this and the bus drove on. Instead of policemen arriving, instead of a crowd collecting, instead of bitter words and recriminations, collecting of evidence, witnesses, etc. – all was smoothed over by the delightful temperament of the victimized man!

Presently I observed that we were entering upon more spacious and imposing thoroughfares, and a little afterwards I noticed

that there was a river on our right, very much like our own River
Thames. This seemed to interest the *Nacirema*, who had been
silent for some time.

'Say, Bo,' he said at last. 'You don't call this little dribble you've
got here a river, do you? Why, back in my countree, we've got
what you'd really call rivers.'

The conductor did not reply directly to this. Instead he leaned
again out of the window, and shouted to the driver.

'Say, Bert,' he cried. 'Your radiator's leakin', ain't it?'

Even this piece of withering sarcasm did not have the desired
effect of subduing the *Nacirema*, who seemed to have some
extraordinary critical kink in his brain as regards the *size* of
everything he saw. There happened to be an old lady sitting next
to him, who was carrying a shopping basket on top of which was
perched a large melon. I noticed him looking at this in a curious
way for some time, and then he spoke again.

'Say, Bo,' he said. 'Would you folks on this side call that there
lil' fruit a melon? Why, back in my countree, I guess we got
*lemons* bigger'n that.' And he picked up the melon to scrutinize it.

'Arfamo, chum,' said the conductor. 'Put down that *grape!*'

I may say here that in Moribundia the *Nacirema* is driven by
some urge in the depths of his being to show his worst side and
make his most oudandish statements whenever he is in the presence of a *Yenkcoc*, and that in the verbal encounter which ensues
he invariably gets the worst of it. But then it is an axiom there that
no one can ever get the better of a *Yenkcoc* in a verbal argument.

I would only weary my reader if I recounted all the exchanges
which now passed between these two, or the countless other
absurd things which were uttered or enacted during the remainder of the journey. I think, however, that the episodes I have
given furnish very fair examples of the general type and level

of the humour and behaviour one is certain to encounter in a Moribundian bus drive. I only wish I could have brought back with me some copies of the well-known Moribundian newspaper, the *Gnineve Swen*. This deservedly popular paper gives columns daily to the narration, by its readers, of these deliciously funny little episodes illustrative of the *Yenkcoc Ruomuh* – which it certainly could not do unless there was a virile demand for it, and which goes again to prove how dear this extraordinary figure, the *Yenkcoc*, is to the hearts of all true Moribundians – whether it be for the reasons I suggested above or not.

About ten minutes later we came into a thoroughfare very closely resembling our own Oxford Street, and something told me we were in the centre of the town, and that it would be advisable for me to get off the bus. I was trying to make up my mind, looking out of the window at each stop, when all at once something happened, or rather I saw something, which nearly shot me out of my seat.

The gloriously pretty girl who had so fascinated me on entering, had moved over to a seat opposite to me, and had been looking out of the window so that I could only see her profile. She now turned and looked at me, and I saw her full face for the first time.

I do not know how to express the macabre horror of what I saw. It was not one face, but two faces in one! A straight, firm dividing line came down from the middle of the forehead, through the nose, to the chin, and it seemed that each half of her face belonged to a different person! While in the left side of the face I recognized the lovely creature I had before seen, the right side belonged to an old, vindictive, hideous hag! – a hag, moreover, whose skin was disfigured with such atrocious blotches, pimples, blackheads, wrinkles, wens, creases and spots that I still feel almost sick in writing about them. No horrible monster envisaged in ancient mythology, no crazy invention of a diseased modern surrealist, could approach in sinister terror this hag-maiden, this half-witch-half-girl looking at me in an ordinary bus – venomously with one eye, an angelic beam in the other!

I shall attempt to give an explanation of this extraordinary phenomenon later in this book. At present I shall merely note that it put an end to any hesitation I had in the matter of getting off the bus.

# CHAPTER FIVE

I myself am by now so familiar with the names of the main streets and thoroughfares in the centre of the Moribundian capital – *Drofxo Teerts, Yllidaccip, Tneger Teerts, Elbram Hera, Mahnettot Truoc Daor, Raglafart Erauqs* and the rest – that I find it extremely hard to realize that they can convey nothing at all to the mind of my readers. For the moment, however, we will have to put up with this disadvantage, as it would be most inconvenient at this point to launch upon any detailed topographical description of the *Nwotsemaht* scene. I shall make do with saying that the general appearance of the architecture and layout was very similar to our own West End – though there were, of course, vital differences in detail and in the physical appearance of the pedestrians which will be described in due course.

Actually, the point at which I had fled from the bus was *Drofxo Sucric* – a point at which four roads, all teeming with traffic, meet. I took at random a road leading in a southerly direction – *Tneger Teerts*, a famous Moribundian shopping centre – and as I walked along I tried to decide upon my best plan of action.

I was now pretty exhausted and felt that I must have a rest, a meal, and, if possible, a bath, before I made up my mind to anything else. But for any of these I should have to go to a hotel, and how was I to go to a hotel without any baggage and with only English money in my pocket?

I at last decided upon a bold plan. Tired as I was, it was

necessary for me to summon up all my remaining strength and courage, and bluff my way through. I must go to a hotel, say that my luggage had been in some way delayed, or was coming on immediately, and hope that my general appearance and carriage would win the day for me. At least I might get a night's rest and a meal in this way – the morning would have to look after itself.

The question remained – at what sort of hotel would such a ruse be most likely to succeed? I soon decided that I must go to the best and largest I could find – something run on impersonal lines where as little interest as possible would be taken in me as an individual. Besides, I was wise enough to know that if one is going to bluff at all it is best to do it in a big way.

Coming to the end of *Tneger Teerts*, passing through *Yllidaccip* and then on through a place known as *Retseciel Erauqs*, I had so far seen nothing I thought suitable. But in a few moments I came upon a vast open place with a column in its middle, *Raglafart Erauqs*, and leading from this in the direction of the river (the River *Semaht* itself) was a wide avenue, one of whose sides consisted almost exclusively of hotels of the larger and more imposing kind.

One of these – called simply 'The Moribundian' – I chose, and walked, with as nonchalant and bored an air as I could muster, through its great revolving doors, into its enormous and shining lobby, and up to its sumptuous desk.

The clerk, at the moment of my arrival, was so engaged with some correspondence at a desk behind the counter that he failed at first to see me. As my fate largely depended upon how this young man summed me up, I looked at him with particular interest. He was a good-looking young man of about thirty, and dressed with scrupulous neatness; but he had such a haggard, livid, overworked, exhausted, tense expression that one at once felt quite sorry for him. The mere fact that he had not seen me was proof that he was at the moment not fully capable of doing his duties properly, and the miserable way in which he looked at the mass of papers in front of him told the same story.

He still showed no signs of having seen me, and I was wondering what I could do to attract his attention, when all at once there entered, from a door at the back of the bureau, another man, as sprucely dressed as the clerk, but considerably older and less attractive. His head was bald on top – he wore pince-nez and a small moustache and there was a mixture of meanness, arrogance, and fury in his expression which was most repulsive. That he was going to address the clerk in angry tones was clear enough – as it was also clear enough that he was in a position to do so – that he was a manager, or at any rate under-manager of some sort.

I do not know whether the reader will believe, or even be able fully to understand, what now took place. I can only swear that it is the truth, and describe it as well as I can.

The manager had just reached the clerk, and I was expecting to hear a torrent of words – when nothing of the sort happened. Instead, there was a sort of blinding flash of white light (such as you might get in flash photography) and, pouring forth from the manager's mouth, like steam, there was made visible (three or four times bigger than the manager himself, and, like the rays from the bus-driver's nose, completely blotting out all the scenery behind it) what I can only call a vast sheet of illumination in the shape of a balloon. And on this 'balloon,' this white frozen steam, this mystic yet seemingly material emanation, words, ordinary words with ordinary punctuation marks, were printed for all the world to see!

I can only express this by some sort of illustration. Here is the balloon, with the words it contained, as it belched forth from the mouth of the manager, who was leaning over the clerk with the furious expression of which I have spoken:

HERE'S A FINE STATE OF AFFAIRS, MATHERS! OLD LADY GRANDLEIGH IS FINELY RUFFLED AT YOU PUTTING HER IN THE WRONG ROOM! . . . HAS BEEN COMING TO THIS HOTEL FOR THE LAST FIFTEEN YEARS TOO . . . SAYS SHE CAN'T UNDERSTAND THIS "MODERN INCOMPETENCE" . . . AND THIS IS THE THIRD MISTAKE OF THE KIND YOU HAVE MADE TODAY! WHAT HAS COME OVER YOUR WORK LATELY? ARE YOU ILL OR SOMETHING? WE DON'T WANT SLACKERS OR MUDDLERS HERE. IF THE "PACE" IS TOO FAST FOR YOU WE SHALL HAVE TO MAKE OTHER ARRANGEMENTS —THAT'S ALL. I WILL SAY NO MORE THAN THAT, BUT I HOPE YOU CAN TAKE A HINT!

MANAGER'S MOUTH

The clerk, without looking up or relaxing his harassed expression, replied to this lengthy statement with a balloon of his own. In point of fact, this balloon was discharged simultaneously with the manager's, so that a curious impression was given of their rudely talking in competition with each other, without hearing what the other said or caring to hear it. From the nature of the clerk's reply, however, I was led to believe that there was some tricky Moribundian time-factor – which my earthly wits were not quick enough to follow – and that the clerk must have heard all that the manager had said before launching upon a statement of his own point of view. This is what came pouring from his mouth:

> ALL RIGHT, SIR—ALL RIGHT—DON'T GO ON AT ME! I AM SORRY ABOUT OLD LADY GRANDLEIGH—BUT SURELY A CHAP CAN MAKE A MISTAKE ONCE IN A WHILE. THESE RICH PEOPLE, WHO LIVE A LIFE OF LEISURE, DON'T SEEM TO UNDERSTAND THAT . . . I DON'T KNOW WHAT'S THE MATTER LATELY— EVERYTHING I TOUCH SEEMS TO GO WRONG.

CLERK'S MOUTH

These two balloons remained in the air for about as long a time as it would take an educated person to read them both conveniently – then they faded, and the objects which they had obscured were again visible. The manager, having delivered his warning effectively enough, withdrew through the door by which he had entered without any more words – or I suppose I should say balloons – while the clerk went on with his work.

I hoped now to get some attention. I was just about, in fact, to raise my voice to make my presence known, when, taking me completely by surprise, there was another bright flash, and yet another balloon hung in the air. This came from the clerk again, but was different from the one that preceded it, in that, instead of flowing out of his mouth as before, it burst, as though from some astounding inner explosion, from the very brain of the man – piercing the thickness of his skull, and coming out through his hair, to hang in the air with the utmost brightness and legibility.

That this balloon represented what the clerk was thinking, as opposed to the other balloon, which had represented what he was saying, was made doubly evident. Not only did it issue from his brain, which in my opinion made the difference perfectly clear without any further emphasis, there was also additional aid given to the 'reader', if I may call him so, in the form of an explanatory heading, or caption, placed at the top of the balloon itself, and leaving no room for misunderstanding even in the slowest-witted mind.

This is the clerk's second balloon as I read it:

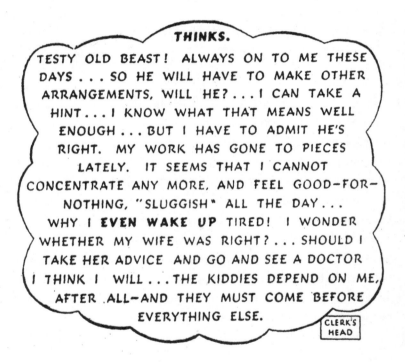

**THINKS.**

TESTY OLD BEAST! ALWAYS ON TO ME THESE DAYS . . . SO HE WILL HAVE TO MAKE OTHER ARRANGEMENTS, WILL HE? . . . I CAN TAKE A HINT . . . I KNOW WHAT THAT MEANS WELL ENOUGH . . . BUT I HAVE TO ADMIT HE'S RIGHT. MY WORK HAS GONE TO PIECES LATELY. IT SEEMS THAT I CANNOT CONCENTRATE ANY MORE, AND FEEL GOOD-FOR-NOTHING, "SLUGGISH" ALL THE DAY . . . WHY I **EVEN WAKE UP** TIRED! I WONDER WHETHER MY WIFE WAS RIGHT? . . . SHOULD I TAKE HER ADVICE AND GO AND SEE A DOCTOR I THINK I WILL . . . THE KIDDIES DEPEND ON ME, AFTER ALL—AND THEY MUST COME BEFORE EVERYTHING ELSE.

CLERK'S HEAD

In due course this faded away, but the clerk did not look up; finally I was compelled to rap upon the counter to make him aware of my presence.

He heard me, and as he rose and came towards me with his harassed and subdued expression intensified by his recent clash with the manager, it occurred to me that I was in a position to adopt a high-handed tone, and that this, in fact, would be my best strategy.

Imagine my surprise when just as I was framing the words in my own mind the words were literally taken out of my own mouth, and I found myself making a balloon of my own!

In Moribundia it isn't altogether a simple matter to read one's own balloon, as they are primarily meant for other people's consumption, and one can only get a sort of sideways, squinting, elongated view of one's own. The thing can be done, however, and this is what I saw myself ballooning:

WHAT THE D---L IS THIS! CAN I GET NO ATTENTION HERE? I HAVE BEEN WAITING FOR THE LAST FIVE MINUTES AND NO ONE HAS TAKEN THE SLIGHTEST NOTICE OF ME; IF THIS IS THE SORT OF THING THAT HAPPENS, I SHALL NOT COME HERE AGAIN IN A HURRY!

MY MOUTH

It may be observed that a d, a dash, and an l, quite involuntarily on my part, were substituted for the word 'devil' at the top of this balloon. An automatic and vigilant censorship of this sort takes care of all balloons in Moribundia, which, in certain departments of life, is extraordinarily squeamish with regard even to the mildest forms of profanity – while in others – in the case, for instance, of retired colonels, elderly people whose corns or bunions have been trodden upon, or the owners of barges or small craft – it countenances swearing of the most violent kind. Indeed, to question the habitual use of bad language by such members of the community as these, would be to incur the same sort of displeasure as one would bring upon one's head in questioning the 'unfailing good humour' of the *Yenkcoc*.

The clerk now replied with a brief, miserable, apologizing balloon, and after that we resumed normal speech. I asked for a single room, and the man was so distraught by his own worries that he completely failed to notice that I had no luggage, and, having asked me to sign the register, simply told a page-boy standing near to direct me to my room.

'Here's a bit of luck for me!' I thought, and looked quickly and nervously into the air around my head to see that the thought had not broken into the air to betray me. Happily, it had not. I entered the lift, and a few minutes later was in a luxurious bedroom on the third floor.

# CHAPTER SIX

Having sent out a page to buy me a toothbrush, razor, and other immediate necessities, the first thing I did was to have a bath and wash off the dust of travel through some billions of miles of space! I could hardly speak too extravagantly of the sense of relaxed joy and comfort I extracted from lying back at last in the hot water, and gazing at the green-tiled and beautifully-appointed bathroom.

The boy returned as I was drying myself. I told him that the expenses he had incurred were to go down to my account, and I cunningly led him to believe that he would be getting his tip at a later date. Then, deliciously refreshed by the bath, and exhilarated by the success of my tactics, I began to shave and dress and to look forward to my dinner.

It was now after seven o'clock, and quite dark outside. I made myself look as smart as possible, being thankful for the fact that I was wearing a dark and comparatively new suit, and when I had done I looked in the mirror and thought I would pass.

Though a timid spirit prompted me to sneak pryingly down the stairs, and so avoid any too close contact with any more hotel employees or officials in the lift, I took myself in hand and rang the lift bell with the firmness of a guest with nothing to hide, and meaning to make full use of the amenities of the hotel. I was awarded by the lift-man looking at me in the most satisfactory way possible – that is, apathetically and without seeing me – and I was whizzed smoothly downwards to the ground floor.

It is in keeping with the general character of Moribundia, which, as I have said, is the land of ideals made concrete, that its hotels are everything that they proclaim themselves to be. Up there, if a hotel calls itself the 'Grand,' the 'Splendid,' the 'Royal' or the 'Palace,' it is because it is, in cold fact, really grand, really splendid, or really furnishes an appropriate setting for kings and queens. The 'Moribundian' seemed to be all three. I do not think I can give the reader any adequate idea of the magnificence, the breadth, and the height of the public rooms, nor the splendour and richness of the fittings, the hangings, the chairs, the sofas, the chandeliers, the carpets. All had the quality of something seen in a dream.

Before going to dinner I went and sat in a great drawing-room leading out of the main lobby, boldly ordered myself a cocktail, and had my first look at the other guests. That these all belonged to the upper classes was shown not only by the way in which they were dressed, but by their mere physical outlines, which were all of that slim, elongated, willowy character I had observed in the parents at the school cricket match. Normally, as I have said, this is the great distinguishing feature of the Moribundian 'gentle' class, whilst lack of inches and an uncouth squatness distinguish the 'lower' orders: but in a first-class Moribundian hotel of this kind even the servants are tall and willowy like their betters, and fit in with the scenery. The waiters, particularly, have the most elegant figures and can be seen standing about in the distance in the most graceful attitudes.

My attention was soon diverted by a strange scratching noise coming from the other end of the room. I turned my head in that direction, and saw that the noise was made by a large but extremely beautiful and luscious girl in evening dress, who was writing a letter. I was surprised that I should have heard the noise of her pen so clearly from so great a distance – but this was nothing to my amazement when I discovered the cause – for the piece of notepaper on which she was writing was almost as large as the whole upper

part of her body! Her handwriting was gigantic in proportion
to this stupendous sheet (more like a poster than anything else),
and how she had contrived to form the characters with the pen of
normal size which she held in her lovely hand, I do not know.

She had now stopped writing, and was holding up a finished
sheet; running her eyes over it before she went on to the next. A
vivid idea of the size of the notepaper and her handwriting may
be gathered from the fact that, although I was some twenty yards
distance from her, I could read what she had written without the
slightest difficulty. This is what I read, and roughly how it looked:

ignominious falls, my dear, but nothing
serious! So we have put away our skis
till another year, and returned to town
where Bill (who had sworn he was going to
economize, poor darling!) has insisted on
installing me at the "Moribundian" —
easily the most expensive and exclusive
place in town, and where we at once bumped
into old Lady Grandleigh herself!
Bill (nasty masculine creature) has no
sympathy for my aches and pains acquired
in the 'sacred name' of winter sports, but is
a perfect darling in other ways. As soon as
we arrived he sent out for a huge box of my
beloved Siljoy Stockings — you know — the
ones with those delicious silk threads which
are so soft you can hardly feel them! As it
Bill certainly understands women. As it
happens these Siljoy Stockings are a genuine
economy too. So I could not scold the
poor boy for his extravagance on this
occasion! You must really ask Jack to

There was something so extraordinarily fascinating in the sight of a beautiful young married woman exposing her correspondence and private affairs in this way, that I could not take my eyes off her, and eagerly awaited the moment when she would hold out the next page for inspection. To be perfectly frank, I had a base hope that even more intimate and possibly lascivious details might be exposed to my view; but I waited in vain. Though she continued to write, she did not lift another sheet in that convenient way, and I soon became aware that a singularly handsome, large, and virile young man in evening clothes, sitting a little apart from her, was looking at me resentfully. This, it dawned upon me, was 'Bill' himself, and it did not take me long to decide that if I went on staring at his wife there would be serious trouble. I hastily drank up my cocktail and went into the dining-room.

This was built on the same magnificent scale as the other rooms, was brilliantly lit, and crowded with brilliant people. I was, in fact, at first quite bewildered by the dazzling quality of the illumination, which was derived, I soon realized, not only from the liberal use of electricity, but from the constant flaring up and subsidence of word-balloons and thought-balloons from the mouths and heads of nearly all the people sitting at the table.

I should here state a curious fact about the Moribundian practice of ballooning. Although the Moribundians are liable to give vent to their feelings and thoughts in this way in almost any circumstances, it is noticeable that in the vicinity of food, or seated around any sort of table at which another person or people are seated, and at which a meal is being served, their innate tendency to ballooning seems to receive some kind of abnormal or additional stimulation. Children, old people, young people, aunts, uncles, servants, friends, all are stirred in the same way in the presence of a white table-cloth – whether it be laid for breakfast, lunch, tea, dinner or supper, and pop off their balloons with the prodigality and inconsequence of schoolboys with Chinese crackers.

Imagine then, the effect, as of some harmless yet dazzling indoor pyrotechnic display, of a room in which there were, instead of merely one, at least fifty tables and table-cloths, all surrounded by people. I do not mean to suggest that these people were communicating with each other solely by means of balloons; there was as much conversation and hubbub as you might hear in any crowded hotel dining-room; and I myself, at the small table for one which I was lucky enough to find vacant, communicated my wishes through the medium of the spoken word alone to the waiter, who replied to me verbally throughout.

While I was in Moribundia I made a fairly exhaustive study of this fascinating subject of ballooning – devoting to the task the same qualities of patience and care as would be given to any other form of research. I even went so far as to try to discover some general law lying behind these weird manifestations, and some explanation of the mystery which causes the Moribundian to speak in balloons at certain times and on certain subjects, whilst at other times, and on other subjects, he is satisfied with ordinary speech. Without complacence, I think I may say that my labours were crowned with no small measure of success. Were I to give these results in full, of course, I should be compelled to write a separate treatise on the subject, which I may decide to do at a later date: but in the present work, where my principal aim is to portray the main sociological and psychological aspects of another world, my best plan will be to make do with one or two general observations upon a topic which cannot be said to be of major importance.

I found, then, that balloons could be divided into three or four great families, or categories, all of which are indirectly related to each other. The most prominent of these is undoubtedly the simple 'Fatigue' balloon, a fine example of which was given by the clerk in the lobby. Next, I think, comes the 'Washing' balloon, which takes its source in the persistent use, by Moribundian housewives, of old-fashioned methods of scrubbing their linen, and which is for that reason quite closely akin to the 'Fatigue' balloon. There is then the 'Complexion' balloon, very much in evidence, and also frequently, though by no means necessarily, the result of fatigue. Finally, amongst these major balloon families, is what I can only call the balloon of 'Inexplicable Repulsiveness,' which I shall try to explain later.

Rough and ready as this classification is, it may give the reader some idea of the *type* of ailment or inconvenience which is almost certain to bring a balloon from the mouth or head of the average Moribundian. I suggest that they feel so strongly on certain matters that, just as a man at the point of death (some people say) is able to make himself visible to his distant friends, so they, under the stress of their emotions, can produce these extraordinary projections in the air.

I have mentioned only the major balloon families; there are hundreds of minor ones, naturally; and there is no limit to the amount and multitudinous variety of balloons to be met with in any given family.

I now propose to conclude this chapter by presenting to the reader, with appropriate comments, a number of balloons, or rather balloon-situations, or balloon-dramas, selected from the hundreds I witnessed that night as I ate my beautifully-cooked dinner in silence. I do this at the risk of holding up the flow of my narrative, but no mental picture of the Moribundian scene can be adequately formed without some knowledge of the contents and style of these ubiquitous pieces of printed gas, and if I introduce them to the reader now, at the moment when they were first introduced to myself in full force, I shall be saved the trouble of explanations and comments later.

Though balloons for the most part deal with matters of serious or critical moment in the balloonist's personal life, there is a certain amount of light, amusing, even frivolous ballooning, and an example of this was provided by a young couple sitting a few tables away from me. Before I had finished my hors-d'oeuvre I had come to the conclusion that they were deeply in love with each other, the man, perhaps, being a little more smitten by the girl, than the girl by the man. He was enraptured with her. I noticed, however, that instead of gazing into her face, like the ordinary lover, he was incapable of lifting his eyes from her hands, which seemed to rivet his fascinated attention to the exclusion of all her other charms. At last he could contain himself no longer, and, taking her slender finger-tips in his own, he ballooned in the following manner:

WHAT BEAUTIFUL, SOFT, SMOOTH HANDS! THAT WAS WHAT FIRST ATTRACTED ME TO YOU MY DEAR. WHY, IF THIS WERE NOT A PUBLIC PLACE, I SHOULD SMOTHER THEM WITH KISSES, HERE AND NOW! THEY ARE SO CREAMY AND DELICATE. I CANNOT TAKE MY EYES FROM THEM. YOU WILL COME OUT WITH ME EVERY NIGHT THIS WEEK, WON'T YOU?

To which, with a pleased tolerance towards this minor sexual perversion, or fixation on his part, and dealing in the correct order with the points he had raised, she ballooned back:

> YOU FOOLISH BOY! PEOPLE WILL SEE YOU! MY HANDS ARE NOT SO WONDERFUL — ANY GIRL MAY HAVE THE SAME IF SHE TAKES PROPER CARE OF THEM. YES, OF COURSE, I WILL COME OUT WITH YOU, IF YOU WISH IT.

At the same time a balloon burst from her head, thus:

> THINKS
> IF ONLY HE HAD SEEN THEM A MONTH AGO! WHAT A LOT I OWE TO "SMOOTHALL SOAP." IF BETTY HAD NOT PUT ME ON TO IT I SHOULD NOT BE HERE NOW!

As I read these balloons off, I was quite infected by the happy and idyllic feeling imbuing them. No sooner had they faded, however, than the girl turned away from her lover, and, as though addressing an audience in my direction and seeming to grow somewhat larger in size as she did so, introduced a firmer and more serious, almost a bluestocking note, in the following balloon from her mouth:

YOU TOO, CAN HAVE BEAUTIFUL SOFT WHITE HANDS LIKE MY OWN! SCIENTISTS HAVE SHOWN THAT ALL UGLY DISFIGUREMENTS OF THE HANDS ARE BROUGHT ABOUT, ORIGINALLY, BY INSUFFICIENT WASHING, WHICH SETS UP, IN THE LONG RUN, A CONDITION KNOWN AS "MANUAL UNCLEANLINESS". THIS IS CAUSED BY CERTAIN MINUTE PARTICLES OF DUST, FLOATING EVERYWHERE IN THE ATMOSPHERE AROUND US AND KNOWN AS "DIRT", ADHERING TO THE SURFACE, OR 'OUTER LAYER' OF THE SKIN, AND THEIR BECOMING CONGEALED. THIS MAY LEAD TO SERIOUS CONSEQUENCES IF NOT TAKEN IN TIME. THE ONLY WAY TO ENSURE THE SAFE AND EFFICIENT REMOVAL OF THESE DISTRESSING DUST PARTICLES IS TO EMPLOY REGULARLY A LUBRICANT CAKE SUCH AS IS PROVIDED BY "SMOOTHALL SOAP" WHICH IN ADDITION TO ITS PARTICLE REMOVING PROPERTIES IMPARTS A SOFT, WHITE APPEARANCE TO THE SKIN. USE "SMOOTHALL SOAP" AND SAY GOODBYE TO "GREY HANDS" FOR EVER. YOU TOO CAN BE "BOOKED" EVERY NIGHT!

My next selection furnishes a good example of what I would call a 'transitional' balloon in the category of 'Inexplicable Repulsiveness.' This was originated by two young men, in flawless evening clothes, talking over their dinner. The first threw out a casual balloon as follows:

> YOU'RE A GAY FELLOW, AREN'T YOU? WHO WAS THAT DASHED PRETTY WOMAN I SAW YOU MONOPOLISING THE OTHER NIGHT AT THE HOTEL DANCE? I ONLY SAW HER FROM A DISTANCE, BUT SHE LOOKED A STUNNER. BUT I HAVE NOT SEEN YOU ABOUT WITH HER SINCE. HAVE YOU DROPPED HER?

To which the second replied:

> YES — PRETTY ENOUGH IN ALL CONSCIENCE — BUT PRETTINESS ISN'T EVERYTHING, YOU KNOW. YOU SAY YOU SAW HER FROM A DISTANCE ---WELL IT IS HARD TO PUT, BUT-ER- REALLY -ER — ... WELL-SHALL WE SAY THAT SHE WOULD LOSE NOTHING IF SHE PAID A VISIT TO HER DENTIST?..

These rather offhand and conceited young men were too careless to trouble whether or not they could be overheard and actually the lady they were talking about was sitting at the very next table. She bore every trace of being a beautiful woman, but her woebegone and horrified expression at the moment did not show her off to the best advantage. Two balloons burst from her. One of these was interesting, as it contained no words, but was filled merely with a colossal note of exclamation, thus:

while the other was a brief mouth-balloon:

THEY ARE TALKING ABOUT ME!

This is called 'transitional' ballooning because the problem of the subject's mysterious repulsiveness to men is in the process of being solved.

I can do no better than to follow this by some specimens of the pure 'Washing' balloon in its ultimate stage. These were thrown off by four people sitting at a large table some distance away – a fat, elderly, prosperous-looking man, his wife, also stout and prosperous-looking, but with a kindly and capable appearance, and a young couple, well dressed, but bearing the slightly subdued and deferent demeanour of people who have yet to make their way in the world. I may say that only an experienced balloon-reader would be able to see at once that this *was* Washing' ballooning.

All four had balloons going at the same time, and I will begin with that of the older man, which was directed towards the younger man, next to whom he was sitting:

> Yes, young man, I have decided to give you that post we were talking about last week. A lot of entertaining will go with it, as you know, and it seems to me that you are the man for the job.
>
> I may say that I have been wavering and that my final decision was reached by the appearance of your charming wife. Nothing is so essential as a smart, bright appearance, in bringing in the customers. Your salary, of course, will be substantially increased. Congratulations young man! And, now let's talk no more business for Heaven's sake! What about a game of golf with me next week...?

To this the young man replied, or rather was simultaneously replying:

> Thank you, Sir. I am most grateful for the trust you are putting in me, and I shall do my utmost to see that it is not ill-placed. I am most happy, too, that my wife has impressed you so favourably. She is a great help to me in every direction... There is nothing I should like better than a game of golf. What is your handicap, sir?...

The reader, by the way, will by now have had time to observe what I was beginning to observe – that in any given balloon-drama, all the participants, however their sentiments may differ, belch forth their opinions in exactly the same handwriting, and in approximate conformation to an established shape and manner.

The two women, meanwhile, were looking in the direction of the men, reading off their balloons in a satisfied way, as though they were sitting at a cinema. The elder woman good-naturedly expressed herself thus:

Golf! What children men are, my dear . . . I may say that my husband, though he would be the last to admit it, invariably takes my advice in all matters relating to his business, and that it was my favourable impression of you which made me feel sure that your husband would be the right man for the post. A woman's importance in a man's career cannot be exaggerated, and unless she can be bright and entertaining after a long day's housework, she will only be a drag on him. How "fresh" you look in that pretty frock of yours. You must tell me where you got it. I hope we will be seeing a lot more of each other now-a-days.

To which the young wife replied by mouth-balloon:

> *Thank you, Mrs. Overbury. I can modestly say that I have always felt it was part of my business to keep bright and fresh for my husband's friends at the end of the day, and the results tonight have exceeded my wildest hopes!*

In addition to this, however, she was slyly sprouting out a balloon from her head. This bulged out well to the right of the group, and furnished a clue to all the others.

> **THINKS**
>
> *And to think that a few weeks ago I was so weary and exhausted after a day's washing that I was snappy and irritable with Jack, refusing even to go out with him to the local cinema! What a difference "SLOOSHALL" has made to my life — and also to Jack's career! Washing, which at one time never took me less than six or seven hours is now achieved in as many seconds by "SLOOSHALL", which is not injurious even to the most delicate fabrics. No more back-breaking days at the tub, no more harsh scrubbing and scouring for me! Even this frock I am wearing, which Mrs. Overbury has taken for new, was washed in "SLOOSHALL", which has, in addition, the supreme merit of being the cheapest product of its kind on the market, and is within easy reach of the poorest housewife's purse*

The reader will by this time have observed what an explicit, conscientious, informative, lengthy affair the average balloon is, and therefore how impossible it is for me, in a work of this kind, to give more than a few examples of the hundreds I watched that night with tireless fascination.

I was, in fact, so captivated by this, to me, so utterly novel method of reading, that I lingered for something like two hours over the table after I had finished my dinner, and presently found myself amongst quite a different crowd of people, who were coming in for supper. Soon I saw tables were being moved from the centre of the room; a carpet was rolled up and taken away; a band appeared and dancing began.

There is a lot of ballooning done on the dancing floor in Moribundia, though, of course, there is nothing of that mushroom-like proliferation brought about by the presence of dining-tables. I cannot refrain from giving, in conclusion, a striking little bunch of three balloons (two mouths and one head) floated by a young couple dancing amidst the blare of the band.

The girl, pretty enough, but whose face looked to me as though it had recently been splashed with black mud from a passing motor car, ballooned naïvely and innocently thus:

To which the young man responded with a halting and evasive balloon thus:

WELL-ER- I DON'T KNOW-ER-YOU SEE-ER-I THINK I OUGHT TO GO BACK EARLY-ER-TONIGHT. ER-WE HAVE BEEN VERY MUCH RUSHED AT THE OFFICE OF LATE, AND I HAVE -ER- SOME WORK TO PREPARE BEFORE TOMORROW. SORRY-ER- PERHAPS SOME OTHER TIME -ER

While in a balloon over his head he revealed what was going on in his mind:

THINKS

WHY!-HER FACE IS ALL COVERED WITH NASTY, DISFIGURING BLACKHEADS, AND BLOTCHY PIMPLES! HER NOSE IS ALL SHINY, TOO!

How it had come about that the young man had not been able to observe the condition of his partner's complexion before he had decided to take her out for the evening, I cannot understand – particularly as the blemishes of which he was belatedly complaining could be seen 'a mile away', as they say. It also struck me as curious that the young woman should be so naively unaware of, or indifferent towards, the fact that her face looked as though it had been splashed with black mud from a passing motor car.

Indeed, at this point, the curiosity and complexity of everything I was seeing and had seen, begun to get the better of me, and I had an unpleasant feeling from which I suffered intermittently throughout my whole stay in Moribundia – a feeling that I was dreaming, that my senses were functioning in a world of realities so preposterous that my human brain could not cope with them – that I could not bear the stress much longer, and yet had no means of escape, of 'waking up'.

I decided that I was dead tired and must go to bed.

I did so, and, leaving whatever weird and wonderful tomorrow that awaited me to look after itself, fell into dark, delicious sleep, almost as soon as my head touched the pillow.

# CHAPTER SEVEN

The room in which I slept had evidently, at one time, formed part of a suite of some sort, for there was a locked door leading from it into the next room. This room, I knew, was occupied by a young man, for I had seen him coming out of it as I went up to bed.

You could hear sounds quite clearly and easily through the locked door, and I was awakened the next morning by the murmuring sound of a voice the other side. I presumed at first that two people were holding a conversation, but I at last came reluctantly to the conclusion that the young man, who had seemed normal enough, was talking to himself.

'Goodness gracious!' I heard him saying, 'it is a quarter to eight already, and if I am to reach that important appointment in time, I have to dress, shave and have my bath and breakfast by eight o'clock! But why should I worry, after all? With this wonderful new method of shaving (here he raised his voice a little) known as *No-ra-zor-o*, I shall be ready in next to no time!'

There was a short pause here, and then he went on, in the same genial, if somewhat complacent manner:

'There! Abracadabra! A perfect shave in fourteen and a half seconds! And no soap, no brush, no water, and no razor – this wonderful discovery – *No-ra-zor-o* – believed by scientists, by the way, to have been used originally in a crude form by the primitive Indian tribes – dispenses with them all! Now I have plenty of time to take everything easily and yet reach my appointment in time.'

He stopped again here and I thought he had finished, but he had not.

'When I think,' he went on, 'of the dreadful scraping and scouring of the old razor method, of all the terrible gashes and slashes I used to give myself, with the necessary grave risk of infection and blood-poisoning, I feel more grateful to *No-ra-zor-o* than I can possibly say. In addition to which, *No-ra-zor-o* contains a certain ingredient believed to have been used in the first place by the ancient Persians, which has a markedly rejuvenating effect upon the skin. Ever since I have been using it, my friends have been telling me how much younger and handsomer I am. Blessings on *No-ra-zor-o*, I say.'

Well, I thought as I listened to this, it was good to know that *somebody* was starting the day in such excellent spirits. I got out of bed and began to dress myself, using the only method of shaving I knew, and with my mind full of problems.

It was not until I came to putting on my coat that my next surprise came. I was conscious of an unfamiliar bulge in my breast pocket, and, putting in my hand to see what caused it, I pulled out a thick wad of no less than twenty-five Moribundian money notes.

I could not imagine how they had got there, or who, if anyone, had played this benevolent trick upon me, but I was not going to let that worry me. For the time being my immediate problem was solved. I would be able to buy all the necessities I required, pay my bill at the hotel, tip, and get about as I wanted.

I should say here that this miracle was repeated every morning of my stay in Moribundia, and that however much I had spent the previous day, there were never less than twenty-five notes in my pocket in the morning. I shall try to give some explanation of this when I come to the question of the creation, appropriation, and distribution of wealth in Moribundia, where the laws governing such things are utterly different from our own, and practically inconceivable by us.

Full of the new-born confidence in myself engendered by this feeling of having an adequate supply of the currency of the country in my pocket, I went down to breakfast in the best of spirits, and gave my order to the waiter with the air of a man born and bred in Moribundia.

There was a good deal of what I call 'breakfast' ballooning going on at the other tables, some of it gay, some of it deeply despondent, and most of it concerned with the matter of the cereal for the first course. Whereas some people wore an exhausted, strained expression, and, putting out despairing balloons, could hardly eat a thing, others were beaming and chatting and swallowing up everything in sight. I, myself, made a good breakfast on the whole, glad of my human power to fall into neither of these extremes. As for the balloons themselves, I was now so used to the sight of them that I don't believe I even troubled to read them all.

After breakfast, I decided to go and have a smoke in the lounge – a decision which was to have a far-reaching effect. For in the doorway to the lounge I accidentally collided with an old gentleman who was destined to play no small part in the history of my sojourn in Moribundia.

This old gentleman had such white and bushy eyebrows, such piercing eyes, such a tremendous moustache, such a vigorous forehead, such a hawk-like nose, such a prominent and pointed chin, and such an expression of general fury and irascibility, that for a long time I was most uneasy whenever I was in his presence. At this particular moment, however, I was genuinely terrified, for it seems that in bumping into him in the doorway, I had had the misfortune to tread upon his foot, and that he happened at the time to be suffering from corns. Back in the world I have never been so unlucky, in a whole lifetime, to place my foot accidentally upon anybody's corns, nor have I actually ever seen this mishap take place in public anywhere; but in Moribundia it is possibly one of the most common forms of misfortune and the victim almost invariably lets out a tremendous yell of agony and protestation.

The old gentleman, however, though he glared at me with an anger so fiery and concentrated that I felt he would burst, mercifully expressed his opinion of myself and the situation in the silence of a balloon. Grateful as my nerves were for his use of this method, I was mystified by the appearance of the balloon itself, which looked something like this:

Which was followed, a moment later, after I had meekly endeavoured to stutter out some form of apology, by one containing no words whatever, being made up exclusively of asterisks, exclamation marks, question marks, and dashes, thus:

He then went on his way. I was looking awkwardly around to see if anyone had witnessed this embarrassing scene, when I saw a charming girl coming in my direction with an apologetic look in her eye.

'You must excuse my father's awful language,' she said, smiling at me in the most delightful way. 'He is a retired colonel, as you can see.'

As a matter of fact, I did *not* quite see at the time, as I did not then know that what I now call an 'asterisk' balloon was the one feature by which retired colonels, majors, and generals in Moribundia might be identified instantly anywhere, even if they were in plain clothes.

I now signified to this enchanting newcomer that I was in no way offended, and after a few remarks about the weather we went over in the direction of the fire-place and, sitting down, fell into light conversation.

This was the first time I had spoken to a Moribundian for any length of time, and at close range, and I was secretly relieved to find that I was 'getting over' all right. She seemed to see nothing odd in me, and conversed in the most polite and unsuspecting manner. True, when I made so bold as to offer her one of my cigarettes (I had bought a packet at dinner

the night before) she did suddenly and rather snubbingly balloon at me:

while taking a cigarette (one made with a special sponge tip) from
a packet of her own, but she at once went on to explain, in the
most minute and painstaking way, how the sponge absorbed all
the smoke, so that none of it got into her mouth, and I could see
that she was not really offended.

In addition to the pleasure I took in finding someone to talk
to, I was, of course, irresistibly fascinated by the physical charms
of my new friend. In fact, I may as well say now that I fell head
over heels in love with her, and I do not see how any man with
blood coursing through his veins could have done otherwise.
It would be impossible for me to exaggerate the beauty of face
and figure, the slimness, litheness, and freshness of the average
Moribundian girl when she is not suffering from any one of those
disfigurements resultant upon the innumerable Moribundian
epidemics. If it had not been this girl, whose name was Anne, I
have no doubt I should have fallen as deeply in love, physically,
with any other girl who took any notice of me. By this, I do not
mean to convey that I am not glad that it happened to be Anne,
or that having fallen in love with her I ever felt any inclination
towards any other girl during my stay up there.

We had been talking for about half an hour, and I had noticed that for some time she had been trying gently to 'pump' me with regard to my profession and standing, when a sudden impulse seized me to throw myself upon the mercy of this lovely creature, and I acted upon it at once. I was too cautious to tell her the whole truth, but instead I invented a vague yet plausible story about myself which I thought would serve my purpose just as well. I told her that I had been 'abroad' for years, living 'in the wilds' – that I had only just returned, and that I was utterly bewildered by the town and did not know my way about or what was what, that my ignorance of civilized things and behaviour was leading me into embarrassing predicaments, and that I should be infinitely grateful if she would give me some assistance until I found my feet.

She accepted this story so guilelessly, asking for no geographical details of my supposed sojourn abroad, and adopting at once so charming a maternal attitude, that I felt quite ashamed of myself. She said she would be only too happy to show me the town; and asked what it was that I wanted to see. I replied that the first thing I had to do was some shopping, to get something in the nature of an outfit, and that I had no idea where to go. She replied that there were plenty of places, and after a little modest hesitation on both sides, offered to come with me to them, if I wished, there and then.

I accepted, of course, joyfully, and about ten minutes later we were out in the street and on our way. It was a fine morning and I felt quite intoxicated with my good fortune. I compared my present walk with my walk to Chandos Street the 'day' before. I had arrived safely, I was staying at a splendid hotel, I had money, I was accepted as an ordinary being by the habitants of this strange world so like our own and so different from it, and I had as guide and friend the most beautiful girl I had ever seen in my life.

She said she would like to enjoy the fresh air by walking to *Egdirrah*, the big store at which she said I could get all I wanted, and I plied her with countless questions as we went along. After a time, however, I saw that I must be a little careful in the sort of questions I asked – there was a certain type of ignorance which no amount of hypothetical isolation 'abroad' could adequately account for.

For instance, we had not been walking long before I saw staggering towards us a middle-aged gentleman leaning heavily on two sticks. His face was contorted in the most dreadful manner, and he was yelling out in agony. The cause of this was not far to seek, for as far as I could see he had some kind of high-powered electric battery concealed under his coat and around his waist, which was causing flashes of jagged lightning to burst forth from his hips.

'Good heavens!' I said to my friend. 'What is the matter with *him*?'

To my surprise she looked at me in a semi-puzzled way. 'What is the matter with him?' she repeated. 'Er – how do you mean, exactly?'

'Why,' I replied. 'What are those flashes of lightning coming from him, causing him such hideous pain?'

'Why,' she said, now looking at me in fresh bewilderment. 'You've seen people crippled with rheumatism before, haven't you?'

'Oh, yes,' I said. 'I see . . . of course . . . yes . . . rheumatism . . . yes . . . how silly of me . . . '

But, of course, I did not really see, as I was not then acquainted with the ghastly aspects which rheumatism sometimes assumes in Moribundia. I was later, of course, to see hundreds of these wretched old gentlemen with pieces of lightning coming out of their waists, and by then it was as easy to recognize a sufferer from rheumatism by his lightning flashes as it was to recognize a retired colonel or major by his asterisk balloon.

Then, a little farther on, a girl passed us who had no nose – this part of her face being replaced by a target. I am aware that I am already speaking in the most placid way of things which will seem incredible or monstrous to my readers, but this is only a reflection of that calm attitude towards the miraculous and the *macabre* which experiences of this kind had forced upon me before I had been twenty-four hours in the place. I say that the girl had no nose, and that a target was in its place. I do not quite know what the reader will make of this statement. I am sorry for him, but I can say no more, and I can say no less. She had a target for a nose, a target with a black bull's-eye in the middle, and a few circles around it, such as you might see at any rifle range (only smaller, as the space for it on her face was naturally limited). I was not near enough, and she passed too quickly for me to see whether it was made of flesh or of wood, or how it had been fixed on, or whether it had grown like that from childhood. In addition to the target there were two huge arrows hanging in the air with their points adhering, by what means of magnetic attraction I have no idea, to the centre of the bull's-eye; and on one of these arrows was written 'Germs,' and on the other 'Infection.'

'I say,' I said to Anne. 'Did you see that girl?'

'Yes, what about her?'

'I mean to say – did you see her nose?'

'Yes – what of it?'

'Well, it was a target, wasn't it?'

'Yes – what about it?'

'But why is it a target, and what does it mean?'

'Why, just that her nose is a target, that's simple enough, isn't it?'

'But why is it a target, and what is it a target for?'

'Why, for germs – for infection. I should have thought anyone could have seen that.'

'But why her's particularly?' I said. 'Isn't everybody's nose a target for germs and infection?'

'Not if you take the right precautions,' she said, and I could see she did not want to go on with a discussion that seemed to her foolish and pointless.

For this reason I made no comment when a few moments later we passed a man whose bronchial tubes and nose, seen in pro-file, were replaced, not by a target, but by a huge tap which was dripping on to the pavement most unpleasantly.

This blending of inorganic with organic matter is one of the most disquieting and curiously repulsive features of Moribundian life. The thing works both ways. Not only do taps, and targets, and suchlike, replace living tissue in the human face; also inanimate objects are constantly taking on human features. I have seen milk-cans, pillar-boxes, lamp-posts, teapots, clocks, and hundreds of other kindred objects, take on eyes, ears, nose, and mouth and grimace in a benign or despondent way. In fact, inanimate things are themselves actually capable of ballooning. I have, even, seen the froth on a glass of beer wink most seductively at its consumer and balloon:

I had made up my mind, then, to ask no more questions about these things, lest I gave myself away too flagrantly. But I had hardly made my resolution before it was too severely taxed by the sight of a young man coming in our direction. He bore exactly the same agonized expression as the old gentleman with lightning coming out of his waist, but in this case his anguish was caused by a band of five or six small devils, or demons, each horned, tailed, and with a three-pronged fork in its hand, flying about in the air around him, and prodding him in the stomach and side, in ecstasies of malicious glee.

'Good God!' I said. 'What are those terrible little creatures tormenting that wretched young man?'

Anne now smiled at me, as though she could no longer take me seriously. 'Of course, I didn't realize you were joking,' she said. 'Are you going to tell me now that you have never seen anyone with indigestion before?'

Indigestion! So that was it! 'Oh, I see,' I said to Anne, and smiled back at her in a way which suggested that I was, indeed, playing a little joke on her, and that I knew well enough that no one in their right senses could fail to recognize a case of indigestion when it was put so plainly before them.

We had now reached the big store to which she had been leading me, and we went inside. I saw that the hosiery department was on the third floor, and suggested we should go up there, and, as we had to start somewhere, commence my shopping by buying some socks. We went up in the lift.

We were a very long time getting served, owing to the fact that the very pretty girl behind the counter was attending to a vast woman with the most dominating appearance and rudest manners I have ever seen. In addition to snubbing the girl in every possible way, and at every possible opportunity, she seemed to have no intention of making up her mind as to what she wanted to buy. There was already a huge pile, or mountain, of material, at least five feet high, upon the counter, and at the moment of our arrival the girl was still pulling down more to add to it from the shelves.

Standing near this formidable and hateful woman, was a little man in a bowler hat, a high collar, pince-nez, and an overcoat too big for him. This little man wore such a meek and harassed expression that I at once felt sure that he was the husband of the woman, and my heart went out to him.

A couple of this sort (unlike, of course, anything ever seen on earth) is a very common sight in Moribundia – the male being known as a *dekcepneh dnabsuh* – a term very difficult to render in English, but meaning, roughly, a man dominated, incessantly scolded, and badgered by his wife. A *dekcepneh dnabsuh* never wears anything but a bowler hat, a high collar, and pince-nez, while the wife is seldom less than three times bigger than her husband. On the surface it would seem that a wretched life is spent by such couples as these – particularly, of course, by the husband – but the latter has an indomitable spirit, combined with certain decidedly mischievous and masculine traits – such as winking at pretty girls, or looking at their legs through opera glasses or telescopes while they are bathing – which give him a satisfaction which may seem exaggerated to the normal man, but which no doubt compensate him for the evils of his domestic life. Also he will quite often go out and get drunk, returning late at night and taking the most elaborate precautions in getting upstairs unheard by his wife, who, on such occasions, waits up in her nightdress to meet him with a rolling-pin taken from the kitchen.

'Er – my dear – er – er—' he now said, seeing that we were

waiting to be served, and employing that hesitant, stuttering, slightly fawning style of speech which characterizes the *dekcep-neh dnabsuh* – 'er – don't you think, my pet – that you might make up your mind – as there are other people waiting to be served, my love.'

'Silence, Henry!' she thundered, and then turned to the girl. 'I don't want any of these, young woman,' she said. 'I have changed my mind and will take half a yard of ribbon.'

There was no withstanding a woman of this sort, and the poor girl, having exhausted herself in hauling out those masses of material on to the counter, meekly complied with this miserable order for half a yard of ribbon. Then, at the roared command: 'Come, Henry!' the husband gathered up a huge mountain of heavy parcels, which practically hid him completely, and stumbled out in the wake of his wife.

I then began my own shopping, which took me something like an hour. Under Anne's guidance I got everything I wanted with the greatest dispatch, and ordered the goods to be sent without paying for them. When we got outside the morning was still young, and the idea of a walk appealed to both of us.

For this purpose Anne took me to a large park, full of trees and greenery and water which lies very near the centre of *Nwotsemaht*.

Towards the end of our walk, and near one of the entrances to the park, we came upon a large open space which was filled by a crowd of people. On approaching nearer, I saw that this crowd was collected around three or four speakers who were elevated above the rest and were haranguing them with violent gestures. I asked Anne what they were speaking about and who they were.

'Oh,' she replied, with an amused and tolerant smile. 'They're not really speaking about anything. They're just letting off steam.' I was curious to hear what they were saying, however, and we approached nearer. I noticed now that each of the orators was mounted upon a wooden box which had once contained soap, wore a dishevelled beard, and exuded an atmosphere of dirt and venom which I wondered the crowd could tolerate. The crowd, however, which was mostly composed of working men of the *Yenkcoc* type depicted by the artist, *Treb Samoht*, was listening with the utmost tolerance and good humour, its members making extremely funny comments from time to time, which were received with delighted laughter.

As to what the speakers were saying, we listened for some time to one of them, and I soon discovered that Anne was right, he was not speaking about anything. In fact, he was talking such extraordinary nonsense, in such an extraordinary jargon, that I find it extremely difficult to remember now and to put it down on paper. I must make the attempt, however, as some knowledge of this subnormal type is most important, as we shall see later, to a proper comprehension of the structure and ideology of Moribundian society as a whole.

'Comrades and workin' men,' I can remember hearing him say, ''oo grind the face of the poor, 'oo sweats the toiler and snatches the bread out of the labourer's mouth? The *capitalists*, comrades, the bleedin' *capitalists!* Dahn with the dirty capitalists, I say, dahn with 'em all – the dirty exploiters! Comrades, our task is liquidate the *bourgeoisie!* Look at 'em, comrades!' Here he pointed to a row of very fine-looking hotels and residential houses that ran alongside the park. 'Look at 'em in their luxury, wallowing in their jewellery and caviare! Look at their cars, their servants, their chauffeurs – idlers all of 'em – never done a stroke of work in their lives. And where do they get their dirty money? From you and I, comrades – the poor starving worker without a shirt to his back. It's we 'oo ought to 'ave the money, and they wot ought to do the work! Everybody ought to be equal! Dahn with 'em, comrades, that's what I say. Dahn with the capitalists! Dahn with the King! dahn with the Constitution! dahn with Parliament! dahn with everybody and everything!'

'There,' said Anne, smiling at me as this illogical and ridiculous peroration was reached, 'there's a *tsinummoc* for you! Shall we go on?'

As we moved on I asked her what she exactly meant by a *tsinummoc*, and she said that she would have thought that the speaker had made that evident himself. But her answer did not quite satisfy me and I asked her whether the word had no political significance of any kind. To this she replied that the actual word did suggest something – advocacy, perhaps, of 'everybody sharing everything with everybody.' This, I gathered, would include women and toothbrushes, and the notion, in any case, was only a screen to hide the unreasoning hatred, fanaticism and bitterness which I had seen.

She spoke of these matters with the same air of calm certainty and wonder at my questions, as she had adopted towards my ignorance with regard to the rheumatism lightning-flashes and the indigestion devils, and it was impossible to doubt the objective truth of her statements. She knew her Moribundia, and I did not.

All the same, I could not refrain from pressing the matter a little further. I asked her whether what she had said was universally true; whether there might not be certain people who genuinely held, perhaps, some milder and more reasonable views on economic equality. To this she replied that such an idea was absurd as no one in their right senses could do so; that it had been 'proved' time and again that such a thing did not 'work'; that in Moribundia it had actually been 'tried,' and shown itself a 'failure.'

She went on to hard facts of Moribundian History. At one time, it seems, in the past, Moribundia *had* made this drastic experiment of sharing out its wealth to everybody, but it had all, after a very short time (according to her), got into the hands of the Jews. And so the scheme was found to be valueless from the very beginning.

Seeing my interest in these matters, she asked if I would like to see an amusing little experiment, in proof of her assertions, which she could perform here and now. We retraced our steps, and listened again to the speaker. Presently he finished, and as he was slinking away through the good-natured crowd, Anne stopped him and slipped a money note (which I saw was for no smaller sum than a thousand pounds!) into his dirty hand. He looked dubiously at her for a moment, glancing suspiciously around to see that no one else had witnessed the transaction, and then moved hastily from the scene.

I asked Anne what all this meant, and she replied, with the same amused smile: 'Now he is a capitalist himself, you see.' She said we would see him again before long, and there the matter, for the moment, was dropped.

In accordance with Anne's prediction, I did see this man again, though, as it happened, I was not with her at the time. I had been in Moribundia about two weeks by then, and had taken a stroll by myself in the park.

I had gone again to listen to these speakers, and was standing on the edge of the crowd, that is, almost in the road, when I heard the soft purring of a motor engine behind me, and turning round saw a huge car, driven by a uniformed chauffeur, and built on the most magnificent and luxurious scale. Sitting in the back, dressed in a frock coat and top hat, and smoking a big cigar (from which the band had not been removed), was a man whose gross and overfed demeanour was so unpleasant as to be almost fascinating. I looked at him for quite half a minute before it slowly dawned upon me that his features were familiar, and before I at last realized that he was none other than the ragged and filthy orator of less than a fortnight ago! Lying back in a plush seat he was looking with a mixture of amusement and contempt at the scene in front of him. I could hardly believe my eyes at first, but as soon as I heard his voice, there was no room for further doubt.

It happened that a beggar passed at that moment and, seeing this ostentatiously rich man, went up to the side of the car and humbly asked him if he could spare a copper.

'Certainly not, my man,' our friend replied. 'I don't believe in encouraging idleness.' He then addressed the chauffeur in the same haughty tone: 'Home, James,' he said, 'and make it quick, or you'll find yourself out of a job, my fine fellow.'

When I related this repulsive episode to Anne, she merely laughed and said: 'I told you so.' She said that it was simply a case of 'Moribundian nature' (which she spoke of in the same way as we would speak of 'human nature'), and that such an experiment could be repeated any amount of times with the same result.

Such is 'human nature' in Moribundia, and incredible as it was I had to accept it, along with all the other marvels and miracles.

In addition, however, to the light which it threw upon questions of the Moribundian character, this episode, properly understood, clarifies much of the whole sociological, economic, and ideological structure of Moribundia, and I feel it is now time that I devoted some attention to these general matters, without some knowledge of which these isolated and somewhat patchy narrations of my adventures as they happened to me can have no fuller significance.

# CHAPTER EIGHT

To begin where it is always wise to begin – in the department of economic facts – it must be understood that in Moribundia wealth is not created by labour.

It may be said that there is nothing remarkable in this, that there are plenty of economists in our own world who can and have described the origin and motions of wealth with hardly any reference to this quality – but in Moribundia the thing goes much further. Indeed, it is true to say that, up there, it would not occur to anyone in their right senses in any way to relate or mentally associate wealth with labour.

What, then, causes wealth in Moribundia, and puts it into the hands of the individual? The answer is known by everyone there – virtue and industry. But by industry I do not, of course, mean an industrial system, objective labour in a social scheme; I mean purely subjective industry on the part of the individual. Those who are virtuous and work hard, make money and get on; those who are bad and lazy, sink into lower social depths. There are no questions of markets, of over-production, of booms and crises to interfere with this unerring and absolute law, to put an excess of money into the hands of the undeserving, or to snatch it from those who have gained it by their virtue and industry.

As the acquiring of money is simply a question of personal merit totally unrelated to any objective facts in the social scheme, it would not be true to say that money is earned in the ordinary way. It simply 'comes'. You have it or you do not have it. It is ideal in origin and ideally distributed. In my case I found twenty-five pounds in my pocket every morning of my life. Apparently, in the working of ideal laws, I was ideally worth just that amount. To me there is nothing extraordinary in this in a land in which people with indigestion are prodded by devils. For all I know, the money may have been put into my pocket by angels or fairies.

One ideal state of affairs creates another. Because there is no conceivable connection in Moribundia between the wealth and the labour of society, it is easy to see there can be no such thing as 'labour trouble'. As we know, the labouring man in our own world, believing, rightly or wrongly, that wealth is somehow caused and created by labour, his own labour, is liable to suppose that he should have a due 'share' of that which he has created, and to make trouble if he feels that he is getting something less than that share. The circumstances being so entirely different, such an idea would never even cross the Moribundian working man's mind.

From this it follows that the Moribundian working man is utterly happy and contented, and this in spite of the fact that Moribundians admit, in fact *insist*, that he is 'always grumbling'. This contradiction is easily understood when one realizes that this 'grumbling' is merely a charming affectation on the working man's part, by which he attempts to screen, but actually reveals, his inner feelings. He grumbles in the same way as one might growl at a child one loved, in excess of affection. If he ceased to grumble he would certainly be less lovable, and it might be taken as a sign that he was less delighted, deep down in his heart, with his lot.

I will not say that there are not certain cases when a Moribundian working man brings a slightly more serious note into his grumbling, as when, for instance, he 'genuinely thinks he has a grouse' – a form of hallucination very similar to that of a hypochondriac who reads a medical book and genuinely thinks he has cancer. Patient explanation and cold facts prove that he has nothing of the kind, and he is quite unable to infect his companions with his pessimism.

In this state of affairs, this relationship, or rather non-relationship, of labour to wealth, is the employer as well off and as happy as the working man? Superficially it would seem that he is not. For whereas to him, as to the working man, money comes according to his personal merit, there is an extra and gratuitous burden on his shoulders all the time – the burden of responsibility. The sum of sleeplessness, worry, and misery caused in Moribundia by responsibility at first sight seems incalculable. In addition to this, or as part and parcel of this, there are the 'risks' he has to take with his money. Moribundian concerns have got to be started somehow and it is the employer's money, owned, remember again, by virtue of his own merit, which has to be risked.

I was puzzled for a long while by this apparent unfairness, but finally came to see that the employer, being what he was, was compensated in other ways. Bred in certain traditions, and educated at schools like the one at which I saw the cricket match on the day of my arrival, he is not the type to shirk responsibility, or to be afraid of living dangerously. To take risks of this sort is nothing to him. He is more than likely to regard it as a privilege. Notice, too, that in shouldering these responsibilities and running these risks, he is automatically acquiring fresh spiritual merit, and therefore increasing his income under the dispensation of the ideal economic law I have already described; and so everything works out and round, in the long run, to a just and equitable state of affairs.

As Moribundia is an economically ideal world in which everybody is economically happy, how is it, you will ask, that a dissentient voice is ever raised, how should such a type as was represented by that man in the park, that *tsinummoc*, have ever come into being, or been allowed to exist? Why should anyone, with no concrete reason, out of the blue, in an ideal state of affairs, of which they are a part, wish, as these people do, to 'sow unrest', to 'spread trouble and discontent', to 'create bad feeling', to 'stir up passions', etc. This is a problem, but I think there is more than one way of explaining it, even if we do not care to remember that there is, and always has been, such a thing as pure evil for its own sake.

In the first place, it is my honest conviction that the Moribundian authorities countenance the existence of these people largely on account of their entertainment value – the fact that they are so excruciatingly funny and keep the working classes amused. As I have already pointed out, there is no quality which Moribundia fosters more carefully or lovingly than the good humour of its working classes, and nothing stimulates this good humour, this spirit of shrewd, robust wit, so well as the spectacle of one of these dotty creatures standing on his soap box and venomously drawing forth from his riotous invention facts and figures concerning a purely imaginary conflict between two purely imaginary classes – the 'proletariat' and the 'bourgeoisie'. Such a one never fails to attract a large audience of working men, and the unanimous enjoyment of all present is a pleasure to see. As a Moribundian once told me, they find it 'better than the pantomime'.

But the thing goes deeper than this, and these people serve another, more serious and educative purpose in demonstrating to the working man the danger of political talk. They can see for themselves either that it leads to madness, or that only mad people indulge in it, and they draw the conclusion that it is best for themselves to keep out of politics altogether.

Are the Moribundian authorities justified in using such measures to isolate the working man from political thinking? From our standards it might seem that they are not, that there is some measure of class propaganda at work here. From Moribundian standards, however, the thing is seen in a different light. In Moribundia there can be no question of duping the working man by discouraging his political thought; there everyone knows there is nothing that the working man detests so much as political thought, that all he desires when he has finished his day's work is, as the Moribundians put it, 'a pint of beer', 'a bit of a chat', 'a pipe', or, perhaps, to 'take his Mrs to the pictures'.

To try and interest him in social matters, then, would be as cruel, tyrannical and meaningless as to make him go and break stones. The Moribundian authorities are, in the truest democratic spirit, merely reflecting his Moribundian will.

But this is not the only reason why, from a Moribundian (as opposed to a worldly) standpoint, social discussion of any sort is looked upon with the deepest disfavour. Social discussion necessarily involves tentative suggestions concerning social change, and towards Change itself, Moribundia, by its very nature, adopts an attitude altogether different from our own. This I must now try to explain.

I have said that Moribundia is the land in which ideals and ideas are made concrete; that is to say, ideas are not brought into being by things; on the contrary, things are brought into being by ideas. Now in our world, where ideas are seen clearly enough to be the reflection of things, so many attempts to understand the nature of things, this opposite state of affairs is not easy to understand. Nevertheless, until we have done so, we cannot understand the true nature of Moribundia. Morals and legislation, for instance, in Moribundia, are not the result of economic and social facts; economic and social facts are the result of morals and legislation. Mind precedes matter; the idea comes first and the reality is made to obey it.

Now, whereas the distinguishing characteristic of things is that they change, and so in our world our ideas, reflecting things, change constantly; the distinguishing characteristic of an idea, isolated from things, is that it does *not* change – it exists in a vacuum, a reflection of nothing, and there is nothing to cause it to change. Consequently, in a world in which things are the blind servitors of ideas, there can be no question of things ever changing. Therefore, to talk of change in Moribundia is to deny everything that makes it what it is, to doubt, and in doubting to threaten, the roots of its entire being, to blaspheme or rave.

Anyone who does this, then, is in Moribundia regarded either as a lunatic or as a person possessed by the spirit of pure, gloating, gratuitous evil – possibly both at the same time. There are, however, such people. In addition to the absurd *tsinummoc* we heard in the park there is a closely-allied type, the *Tsixram*, generally conceived as a more 'intellectual' type, and who may even have been through the motions of having a proper education. According to the *Tsixram* who, as Moribundians say, wish 'to turn the whole of Moribundia upside down', instead of things being the reflection of ideas, ideas are the reflection of things. In fact, according to him, it is quite impossible to deny the fact of change, for, so he says, without change there can be no motion, and without motion there can be no life, no existence. In other words, he has reached the final absurdity of stating that Moribundia does not exist! One may, therefore, regard him as a perfect non-Moribundian, or anti-Moribundian, playing an ideally Satanic role in the scheme of things.

The allusion to Satan is an apt one, for in thinking of that mythical figure we think at once of his rebellion against ideal conditions and of the hell into which he was cast, and over which he became the ruler. There is, it seems, a place in Moribundia – a 'hell on Moribundia', as they say, where the *Tsixram* reigns supreme amidst all the horror and confusion of his wickedness. Concerning this place, which bears the strangely sinister name *Ehtteivosnoinu*, I could not get very much accurate information, as Moribundians, quite naturally, preferred not to talk about it, but that it was a place of punishment of the *Tsixram's* evil, that is to say, a pandemonium wherein his notions and practices reached their logical and terrible conclusion, there can be no doubt. Chaos, starvation, greed, famine, tyranny and a horrible uniformity in the lives of the masses were, as far as I could gather, the prevailing conditions. In addition to this, I understood, everybody was compelled to wear the same clothes and nobody was allowed to laugh.

Again, in this Satan-hell analogy, I observed that just as the Prince of Darkness is reputed to send forth his emissaries into the world to tempt and lure people down into his own region, so disguised devils from *Ehtteivosnoinu* stalk abroad in Moribundia. These 'dark forces', as they are called, are, of course, quite incapable of doing any harm save to the mad, or congenitally wicked, because, as I have said, everybody and every class is ideally happy in Moribundia.

I shall have occasion to allude again to *Ehtteivosnoinu*, but for the present, having explained the bed-rock Moribundian attitude towards Change in general, an attitude which, of course, colours its entire approach to Philosophy, Art, Science and Literature (with which I shall also be dealing later), I think I have cleared the decks for the time being, and can get on with my story.

# CHAPTER NINE

I found my hotel bill in my bedroom in due course at the end of the week, and large as the sum was, it was, of course, well within my means.

I went downstairs to pay it to the clerk – the one, you will remember, who was complaining of exhaustion and in danger of losing his job – but he was not in his usual place at the bureau.

I waited about for a few moments, and then, looking through a door at the back of the bureau, I observed that he was engaged in conversation with a very tall, elderly, clean-shaven gentleman in a frock coat and striped trousers, who looked like a serious statesman of the old school, but who was, I knew, actually no more important a personage than the hotel doctor. He was leaning gracefully against a desk, dangling an eye-glass, while the clerk was sitting on a chair, with a dejected, yet inquiring and dimly hopeful look on his face.

Both were employing the familiar means of expression.

In the background there was a large chart representing the inside and outside of the human body, which the doctor had evidently recently unfolded in order to illustrate his arguments.

The clerk's contribution to the discussion was brief enough, and as I knew something of his condition already, it told me nothing fresh.

I THOUGHT I MUST COME TO YOU, DOCTOR. WHY, I **EVEN WAKE UP** TIRED!

In reply to which the doctor belched forth the following enormous piece of air-printing, one of the largest I ever saw:

POOH—POOH!—A SIMPLE CASE OF WHAT WE DOCTORS CALL "SUB-CONSCIOUS UNDER-FEEDING." YOU ARE PROBABLY NOT AWARE THAT SCIENTISTS HAVE RECENTLY DISCOVERED THAT THE HUMAN BODY, IN ADDITION TO ITS NORMAL FUNCTIONS, PERFORMS HUNDREDS OF THOUSANDS OF ACTIONS DAILY, OF WHICH THE INDIVIDUAL IS COMPLETELY UNAWARE. WHY, DO YOU NOT KNOW THAT THE AVERAGE MAN BLINKS HIS EYES ALONE NO LESS THAN 64,022 TIMES IN THE COURSE OF 24 HOURS, WHILE SUCH ESSENTIAL ACTIVITIES AS SNIFFING, COUGHING, SNEEZING, NODDING, RUBBING AND SCRATCHING CALL FOR AN EXPENDITURE OF DAILY MUSCULAR ENERGY EQUAL TO THAT REQUIRED TO CARRY A WEIGHT OF 347 LBS. A DISTANCE OF 816 YARDS? WHERE IS HE TO FIND THE ENERGY TO REPLACE THAT WHICH IS EXPENDED IN THIS WAY? THAT IS THE PROBLEM WE DOCTORS HAVE TO FACE. IN ORDER TO MEET THESE EXTRA MUSCULAR DEMANDS IT IS NECESSARY TO ACQUIRE THE EXTRA MUSCULAR ENERGY. FOR THIS PURPOSE ORDINARY FOOD AND DRINK IS QUITE USELESS, AS IT IS NOT AN ORDINARY DEMAND. THE ONLY THING WHICH MEETS THE CASE IS **"NOURISHINE"** WHICH I AM CONSTANTLY RECOMMENDING TO MY PATIENTS, AND WHICH HAS THE ADDITIONAL ADVANTAGE OF HAVING A DELIGHTFUL TASTE. YOU MAY EITHER TAKE IT PLAIN, OR WITH THE DELICIOUS "COFFEE" FLAVOUR. THE KIDDIES REVEL IN IT TOO. BUY A TIN AT ONCE AND STOP BOTHERING A BUSY MAN. BE OFF WITH YOU!

When the clerk came out to me I saw that the lines on his face were already less deep, and as he somewhat absent-mindedly gave me my receipt, he head-ballooned:

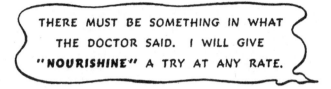

> THERE MUST BE SOMETHING IN WHAT
> THE DOCTOR SAID. I WILL GIVE
> "NOURISHINE" A TRY AT ANY RATE.

At this moment I was joined by Anne, who was paying her own and her father's bill.

My relations with this lovely girl had been a little strained in the last few days, for it had been becoming more clear to me every day that we could not much longer continue to know each other on a basis of mere friendship. I was too much in love with her. On the other hand, I had lacked the courage either to state or even suggest the nature of my feelings, as I did not belong to her world, did not know what she thought of me, and feared that the barrier between us was somehow insuperable. As a consequence of this, in the conflict of my emotions, I had taken to behaving self-consciously in her presence, and even, at times, avoiding her. This morning, for instance, although I could easily have done so, I made no suggestion that she should join me in a walk, and went off by myself in what to her must have seemed a cold or mysterious manner.

I took a long walk trying to make up my mind on this matter, wondering if I dared to approach the subject of my feelings to her, and if so, how it was to be done. I had still come to no conclusions by the time I had got home again. Just before reaching the hotel, however, I happened to pass a draper's shop, in the window of which I saw a box of 'Siljoy' stockings. On the spur of the moment I went in and bought a box.

I saw Anne again at tea-time and presented her with this box. She was delighted with the gift and looked at me in the most tender and, as it seemed to me, significant way, as though I had paid her a rich and meaning compliment of some sort. Shortly afterwards we both went upstairs to dress for dinner, and when I came down again to the drawing-room I saw her seated at a writing-table.

She was in a beautiful satin evening dress, cut very low at the back, and she was writing a letter – looking a vision of beauty in that softly-lit and luxurious setting.

Happily she was using that Brobdingnagian kind of note-paper which I had seen before; and, one of the sheets happening to fall upon the floor, I was able to read what she had written on it from where I was sitting. This is what I saw:

3

most attractively unsophisticated, my dear – has been an explorer, or something mysterious, living in the "wilds" for goodness knows how long. We fell into conversation in the hotel, and have been going about with each other ever since. However, for all his shyness and vague unworldliness, he has a very good knowledge of what constitutes good taste, and how to please a woman most! Why only at tea-time today he offered me a box of those gorgeous 'Silfoy' Stockings – you know, the ones with the delicious threads, which almost drive one mad with pleasure. This has hardly put me into a mood to resist any further advances on his part, which I feel certain are coming! It is odd isn't it, how some men understand women? You really must try and get your Bill to

It will be easy to understand my feelings as I read this, and it dawned upon me that she was referring to me! All my fears and doubts were dispelled at once, and I made up my mind to lay my heart at her feet at the first possible moment.

By a lucky chance her father was dining out that night, and I asked her if she would sit at my table. She readily accepted, and we had the most delightful dinner. I ordered champagne, and in that gay, sparkling atmosphere, with the laughter and the conversation, and the brilliant head and mouth balloons popping off at the tables all around us, I was half delirious with pleasure.

It so happened that I had bought some etchings recently to decorate my walls, and, being anxious to know her opinion of them, I asked her after dinner to come up to my room to glance over them. Well, it will be easily understood that as soon as we got up there, the delight and excitement at finding ourselves alone with each other for the first time was too much for us, and the etchings were not remembered.

It would be quite pointless for me to make any attempt to narrate the conversation which now passed between us – I have no doubt it was as foolish as any other lover's talk. I lit a fire and, drawing up the settee in front of it, we lay back and talked in its friendly light for three hours at least.

It was only towards the end, however, that in a sudden access of emotion I decided that I could deceive this trusting girl no longer and, preparing her as well as I could, and making her swear beforehand that she would keep it utterly secret, I blurted out the facts about myself, my whole story, the whole truth.

I knew as soon as I had done it that I had not made a mistake. My chief difficulty, of course, was to get her fully to believe me, but when I had achieved that, and she was getting used to the idea, she showed, not only that it made no difference in her feelings towards me, but also that she would keep it secret and help me in every way she could. Poor Anne – I think so often of her now – her charm, her directness, her simplicity. Without her collaboration my whole stay in Moribundia, and with it whatever value to science it may ultimately have, would have been a very different thing – undirected, unorganized, difficult, even dangerous. With her by my side, with her to explain each phenomenon as it came along, everything was made almost childishly easy.

She even made a general plan for me that night. She herself was leaving the hotel in a few days, to go into a house in town with her father. The question was where would it be best for me to stay, and we discussed the matter at length.

Finally, at nearly midnight, we parted. I saw her up to her room, which was on the top floor, and in the darkness of the passage, kissed her good night.

As I was about to descend the stairs again, I noticed a light coming from a small room on my right. As I passed the door I looked inside and saw, sitting on the bed, in his dressing-gown, the hotel clerk whom I had seen that morning talking to the doctor. He had a look of satisfaction on his face which I had certainly not seen before, and he had in his hand, and was sipping at, a glass containing a hot mixture which I guessed was the 'Nourishine' the doctor had ordered. As he sipped at this, there appeared – over his head – a little to the left, the following curious rectangular 'balloon', containing two words only and coming from neither the mouth nor the head, thus:

$$\boxed{\text{AND SO} \cdots}$$

In my discussion with Anne that night it had been decided that if I was to make a proper study of Moribundian conditions in the time allotted to me, it would be pointless for me to go on staying at this hotel, where I was only seeing one very limited side of life. It was highly desirable, we decided, that I should get into touch with the intellectual life of the day, to meet the people of moment – the people who 'did' and wrote things, who theoretically understood and were responsible for existing conditions.

For this purpose, she thought, I could do no better than become a member of some good Moribundian club, and thus mix with such people on easy terms. Her father belonged to such a club and she said that if he was approached in the right way, by herself, he could no doubt be prevailed upon to put me up and generally sponsor me.

The next day she got to work on her father, who was introduced to me afresh. Anne made up a wonderful story about myself and my origin, and the simple-minded old soldier accepted everything so readily that I felt somewhat ashamed of myself. In the next few days, under Anne's instruction, I cultivated the old gentleman's goodwill by listening patiently and for long periods to his incessant stories, which mostly concerned his somewhat trivial adventures in a place called *Anoop*, some forty or fifty years ago, and before long, I believe I can say, I had won his heart completely.

He suggested, of his own accord, that I should join his Club;

he took me along there for meals, and, in a fortnight's time things so fell out that I was able to become a member. I at once decided to take up residence there for the time being, and moved in from the hotel.

Anyone familiar with a London club of the better kind will have no difficulty in visualizing the exterior and interior of the same thing in *Nwotsemaht* – which is another way of saying that a London club is itself a decidedly Moridundian institution. The Moribundian club is, of course, as an ideal institution, slightly the better of the two. The space is greater, the hangings and furniture are richer, the silence is profounder, the servants are politer (and more elongated), etc., but otherwise the stranger might notice very little difference externally.

The kind of people that go there, however, and the kind of social atmosphere that reigns there, both differ enormously and yet in a way hard to describe.

The best descriptions of the Moribundian club are to be found in the works of two well-known Moribundian writers, *Nhoj Nahcub*, and *Trebreh Egroeg Sllew*.

In the pages of these writers we hardly ever, if ever, come across the ordinary club member as we know him – that is to say, the listless nondescript individual of unknown occupation, who sits in an armchair reading a newspaper and absent-mindedly scratching himself. On the contrary, almost everyone bears the most distinguished appearance, and is of the first social magnitude.

The level of discussion is correspondingly high and solemn. Lords, Financiers, Bishops, Politicians, K.C.S, Generals, Admirals, Newspaper Owners and Explorers (above all, Explorers) – all meet here to thrash out the problems of the day, in a rich haze of tobacco smoke, informality, and sophisticated, well-bred unanimity. There is nearly always someone 'just down from the House' with the latest news, and again, someone 'just back' from some remote corner of the earth, where he has most probably been engaged on a mission which is almost too danger-ous and mysterious to be mentioned, save in a semi-furtive way, by the others. These last characters, described so perfectly by *Nhoj Nahcub*, are, perhaps, the most imposing characters of all in Moribundian clubs, with their 'lean' bodies, 'tanned' faces, 'whipcord physique' and reserved and steely demeanour. I myself was always slightly afraid of them, as they gave me the impression of knowing almost everything. I knew for a fact that they could speak innumerable foreign languages, including the different sub-dialects thereof (which they could imitate to perfection), and the quantity and quality of their contacts, both at home and abroad, were to me curiously terrifying – it being nothing for one of them to carry on negotiations at one and the same time with, say, 'a little Jew tailor in Belgrade', 'a deaf spectacle-maker in Lima', 'an old woman in a Finnish hut', 'a blind armature-winder in an Estonian ghetto', 'a consumptive professor of Oriental languages in a lesser-known French University', 'a half-paralysed watch-mender in Glasgow', 'a dumb porter in a Swedish brothel', etc., etc. (I am, of course, substituting worldly place-names for the Moribundian.) I think the feeling of fright I had arose from the fact that this far-flung, yet microscopically accurate diversity of information was too closely akin to that possessed by God, who knows, we have been told, whenever the smallest sparrow falls from a tree. But I am digressing.

In speaking of these distinguished types I have made no men-tion of the Moribundian author as met with in the Moribundian club. Much less imposing to look at, in fact rather mean and repulsive in appearance, authors are yet allowed to hover around the talk of the big men, and occasionally to put in a word of their own. But as they are generally 'feminists', or 'pacifists', they are hardly acceptable in such manly company. Also they are nearly always known as 'Little Binks' or 'Little Jinks', or 'Little Spinks' – I don't know why. Such is the atmosphere I now entered for the next two weeks, and a very comfortable, solid, well-fed atmosphere it was. I do not know to this day what exactly was made of me, but I had been introduced by a distinguished asterisk-ballooning soldier, and I presume that I was taken to be an *Akkup Bihas*.

I at once endeavoured, without being too pushing, to make every contact I could, and to enter into every sort of conversation – for here I was amongst the intelligent upper class, the people who did things and were in the know generally, and I was anxious to find out what were the great problems and conflicts of the day, and how they were being solved and fought out.

I had not been at this game long before I began to see I was getting nowhere. Instead of conflicts, debates, arguments, and the legitimate frictions caused by different interests and traditions, I found perfect unanimity existing everywhere on every subject and between every class of person. All the old conflicts, as we know them, such as those between the financial and landed interests, the community and the individual, the Church and the State, militarism and pacifism, politics and religion, science and religion, or, if you like, materialism and idealism, were simply non-existent.

I never met an admiral, for instance, or a general, who was not 'deeply religious at heart'; I never, if it comes to that, met a financier, lawyer, or newspaper owner, who was not 'deeply religious at heart'; while, on the other hand, I never met a bishop or a church dignitary of any kind who did not interest himself in the most lively manner in financial, economic, political, and even military matters, and reinforce his arguments with constant illustrations from such purely material sources. In fact, it would be true to say that the men of affairs occupied themselves almost exclusively with matters of the spirit, while the men of God were hardly interested in anything save material, practical concerns.

Since I have mentioned religion, I should now explain that in Moribundia Religion and Science have been utterly, permanently, serenely, beautifully, touchingly reconciled. We have often been told that this reconciliation has taken place in our own world, but we are always seeing the argument break out in new places; in Moribundia the thing has happened for good and all: there is not even any more talk about it. I should even say that the matter has gone further than mere reconciliation: there is something more than identity of outlook: the two have practically changed places. Just as two lovers, having had a quarrel which they have made up, sedulously compete with each other in casting the blame upon themselves, and so begin a sort of charming new quarrel on a higher plane, so these ertswhile combatants – Science and Religion – in luxurious Moribundian embrace, each vie with the other in avowing the point of view which had once been spurned, and disclaiming the point of view which had once been assumed. Thus it happens that while the churchman's appeal to Moribundia is made purely from the standpoint of Science, from considerations of mathematics, biology, eugenics, psychology, economics, chemistry, astronomy and, above all, physics – the scientist – on the other hand – is almost exclusively concerned with the process of unravelling and discussing the moral order and causation underlying the Universe. While the dreamy scientist gazes fervently on God, the harsh clergyman looks sternly to facts. Seemingly there is the same conflict as before. It will be noticed, however, that it is not Religion which is the loser under this complicated new arrangement.

To understand how this has come about, it is necessary to understand the nature of Science in Moribundia, and the course it has recently taken. This is closely allied to the question of Moribundian Change, discussed earlier, and therefore deserves serious consideration.

To begin with, it must be understood that in Moribundia Science is 'finished'. By 'finished' I do not mean emaciated, done up or worn out; I mean finished in the same sense in which one would use the word in speaking of a schoolboy who has finished simple equations, or French irregular verbs. He is said to 'know' these preliminaries and is going on to something else. In the same way the Moribundians have finished Science.

They were not always in this position – there being two stages in the process – the stage of 'old-fashioned' Science (or 'worn-out theories') and the stage of 'Modern Science' (or 'up-to-date' knowledge). So soon as the Moribundian scientist reached the second stage, he had no higher to climb, he gazed at the world in the plenitude of absolute wisdom – he 'knew' Science.

Religious people in our own world will at once say that there is something irreverent in this – that only God can know everything. But then have I not made it clear that in Moribundia all that claims the scientist's interest is God – that all that he professes to 'know' is God? And what can there be irreverent in knowing God? It is the unique privilege of saints, which is exactly what the really learned Moribundian scientist may be called. This is merely another manifestation of the authentic and logical reconciliation between Science and Religion.

I took great pains to discover at what period this transformation had taken place, when the leap had been made from the old-fashioned to modern science. I was unable to get any exact information, but as far as I could find out, the moment of completion or fruition had happened quite recently, in fact about nine or ten years ago. Otherwise, presumably, it would not have been called modern science but just 'science.'

I had therefore appeared on the scene only a little while, comparatively, after a period of tremendous historical moment – the period in which modern science 'did away' with 'outworn conceptions', 'relegated to the dustbin' all 'old-fashioned modes of thought' and established the kingdom of absolute knowledge on Moribundia.

Now all this is so different from the sort of thing which happens in our world, that the reader will probably find it hard to understand. Down here on earth we are decidedly sceptical of science – most of all modern science. We are aware that what science can give, it can also take away. In its progress and development it renders a certain set of opinions out of date and replaces these with up-to-date ones: but we have no guarantee that its further development will not render these up-to-date opinions out of date, and bring us back to the point where the erstwhile out-of-date opinions are once again up to date. In fact, this is what is invariably happening. When, therefore, we hear of modern scientists to-day speaking of having done away with 'old-fashioned notions of matter' or 'outworn conceptions of time and space', we smile cynically and wait for the next move.

Not so in Moribundia. There they have at last achieved the miracle of reaching a final point; there, when a scientist speaks of 'outworn conceptions' he is believed: they are outworn. In the same way, if he says 'modern science has *proved*' so-and-so, he is not regarded as a fool. In other words, he has found ultimates: which is another way of saying he has found the ideal, the absolute, God. We come round to the same point again.

The reader will now see the connection between the unchangeable nature of Science and the unchangeable nature of the social structure. He will begin to perceive what I was beginning to perceive, that this entire ideal world was based on what I may call 'Unchange': it was ideal because it could not change: it could not change because it was ideal.

I may say that even in the scientific field the *Tsixram* still lurks in the corner, playing his more than ever Satanic role. According to him there is no ultimate knowledge and so no ultimate set of scientific opinions; scientific knowledge is incessantly progressing, and yet also incessantly going back upon itself, or rather turning up as its old self on a higher plane. Such ideas are promulgated in a definite system of philosophy known as *Scitcelaid*, and it is easy to imagine the horror with which they would be greeted, if they were not hilariously laughed at, in this sane and happy land.

It will have been gathered from what I have said that this perfect reconciliation between Science and Religion took place simultaneously with, and was dependent upon, the victory of modern science over the old-fashioned sort. This, of course, is the case. Who, then, was primarily responsible for this reconciliation? There are, of course, many names. Undoubtedly the two outstanding exponents of 'modern' science in Moribundia, however, are *Ris Semaj Snaej* and *Ris Ruhtra Notgnidde* who, under the new dispensation, and for reasons explained above, may really be called saints rather than scientists. Moribundia has not been slow to realize the service they have done (the word 'Ris' itself signifies a title of honour), and their works are practically best sellers. That such a thing should have happened in the case of purely scientific works will be easily understood when one remembers the enormous and far-reaching social implications these works bear.

The scientifically-minded reader may now be saying to himself that although in Moribundia the scientist has changed places and become the saint, the man of God, yet he is still superficially a scientist, and must have put forth specific scientific theories in which he (the reader) is interested.

This is true. But, unfortunately, I had neither scientific training nor sufficient time at my disposal to bring back with me any detailed analysis of the latest (and of course last) discoveries of Moribundian 'modern science'. I can only say that they very closely resemble our own discoveries, but have taken matters considerably further in all directions.

In the realm of physics, for instance (and this I studied principally, for it is in this branch of science that the most spectacular service has been done in the union of Science and Religion), a much profounder understanding of phenomena has been reached by the followers of *Snaej* and *Notgnidde*.

We are quite accustomed nowadays, for instance, in our own world, to the notion that 'matter has broken down into energy'. Such an idea would be regarded as true enough, but as naïve in the extreme up there. In Moribundia matter has not only broken down into energy; it has broken down into morals. With regard to the atom, such amazing advances have been made in the problem of its 'self-determination' that to speak of energy plainly would no longer suffice.

The atom, in fact, began to show such extraordinary variety and nicety of individual choice that it became necessary to think of it in purely human terms. It was even found that it obeyed certain laws of periodic behaviour almost exactly similar to our own – that is to say, it did something very closely akin to 'waking up' in what might quite legitimately be called the atomic equivalent of a 'morning': it performed an act peculiarly resembling the act of 'dressing', proceeded to absorb fresh sustenance in an atomic ritual which we might, without any too great stretch of the imagination, call 'having breakfast', and was then found to move in a certain direction in which its energies increased and it became more actively engaged with its fellow atoms – in short, it had gone to the equivalent of the City. Later, it is found to 'return along a fixed line to the point from which it had started' (to take a train home, in fact), absorb further sustenance, and, after a period of 'etheric receptivity' (listening in to the wireless, undoubtedly), it 'sinks into a phase of immobility and quiescence' – or to put it in unscientific language, it goes to bed and to sleep. This incredible duplication of the familiar diurnal routine is also submerged in a larger scheme as we know it. According to the latest Moribundian scientists the atom undoubtedly goes through the equivalent, over a period of time, of the process of growing up and getting larger: shows very definite electrical preferences for other atoms, and after going through a ceremony of being 'linked' by a third atom, settles down to having the equivalent of children. These are brought up in a variety of ways, and enter – with full personal choice – upon many different careers. Some (*militrons*) go to the equivalent of Sandhurst or Woolwich; others (*nautrons*) are trained for the equivalent of the Navy and defend the Molecule which may be thought of as the atom's Empire. Others again (*scribitrons*) are content to stay at home and work in banks, look after machinery (*mechanitrons*) or, as *mercatrons*, engage in the free competition of the open market. I did not actually come across any scientific work in which it was stated that the average middle-class atom wore the equivalent of moustache, bowler hat, and umbrella, but have no doubt that evidence could be found to this effect.

It is easy enough to see what follows from these discoveries – that if these atoms did not behave themselves in a proper and *orderly* way, if they rebelled against their own established system, if anything threatened their unanimity and moral cohesion – the physical Universe would fly apart. The Universe is, therefore, revealed to be founded upon moral law and order in a new and tremendous sense.

Under these circumstances the question of 'splitting the atom,' so far as I can see, takes on a new significance. To 'split the atom' would be just this – to tear asunder this unanimity and cohesion. This, presumably, is what a *Tsixram* atom would hellishly attempt to do, if there were such a thing and it was able to do so. It would blow up Moribundia in smoke.

# CHAPTER ELEVEN

My attempt, then, to plunge into the vortex of Moribundian intellectual life turned out a complete failure. There was no whirlpool – merely a placid lake of unanimity.

It was at this point, I think, that a feeling of dejection began to spread over me which never thereafter left me, which grew deeper, in fact, every day I stayed in this ideal world, in spite of all I did to combat it.

The earthly reader may not find it easy to comprehend the insidious sort of despair which creeps over one in a world from which all conflict has been removed. Profoundly comfortable as one appears to be, physically and spiritually, under conditions in which there are no money problems, no labour problems, no political or religious problems, one yet finds oneself becoming each day more disquieted in the roots of one's being. I can only describe the feeling as that of being *half-dead*.

After about three weeks of life at the Club, it occurred to me that my growing wretchedness might conceivably be attributable to physical illness. Though normally I am one of the healthiest persons alive, I realized that the conditions in Moribundia were not the same as on earth. In Moribundia there was, all the time, a terrible lot of illness about. There was particularly a countless multitude of illnesses of a minor and irritating nature. One had only to read off the balloons about one to realize this.

An interesting medical problem is raised by this. In an

ideal world one should not expect illness of any kind. I can only imagine that this at one time was so, and that in consequence the people, having lost – or never having had – a normal resistance to ailments such as we acquire on earth, have no strength to throw off these minor afflictions. On the other hand, matters are arranged on a just and perfect basis even here, for it can truly be said that if anyone is ill in Moribundia, or remains ill, it is due to his own folly. For every one of these thousand and one plagues 'modern science' has found a specific remedy furnishing an immediate cure. There are also several remedies and tonics curing *all* afflictions at the same time.

I know now, of course, that my real trouble was psychological; but at the time I suspected that I might, like the clerk at the hotel, be suffering from something I had not suspected, and at last I confided in Anne.

She took the warmest and most charming interest in the matter, having had much illness herself, and, in searching for a satisfactory diagnosis, questioned me closely.

'Do you feel tired?' she said, 'sluggish, "out of sorts"? Do you feel that "everything is too much bother" – that "nothing is worthwhile"?'

I had to admit that this was vaguely the sensation, and she went on eagerly:

'Do you sometimes feel yourself "slipping", that you "can't go on"?' she continued, putting all these mental states into inverted commas, as though she was quoting, and working herself up into what might almost be called a poetic or prophetic frenzy of description. 'Do you get that "full" feeling after meals? Do you feel "snappy", "listless", "irritable", "unable to concentrate"?'

I replied that this seemed to fit the case and, hardly pausing for breath, she went on:

'Do you suffer,' she said, 'from any or all of the following complaints – exhaustion, sleeplessness, nerves, indigestion, loss of appetite, constipation, giddiness, debility, acidity, arthritis, neuritis, lumbago, rheumatism, gout, sciatica, colds, influenza, catarrh, biliousness, headaches, mental fatigue, depression, disordered liver, kidney trouble, sore throat, eczema, baldness, hysteria, ear-ache, toothache, eye-strain, coughing, bad breath, asthma, fainting attacks, shooting pains, palpitation, breath-lessness, anaemia, poor circulation, bad legs, hardened arteries, varicose veins, pimples, boils, spots, etc.? If so,' she wound up, 'you may be certain of a speedy cure.'

Although I had none of these diseases, I did not like to damp her enthusiasm by telling her so, and as the earlier symptoms she had mentioned seemed to resemble mine, I asked her to tell me of the cure. This turned out to be a wonderful discovery known as 'Kewrall', which I could get in tablets. These tablets, she said, contained 'all the natural curative ingredients in concentrated form.' I noticed, by the way, that in Moribundia the greatest store was set by the arrangement of ingredients in concentrated form – it seemed, in fact, the basis of their therapeutics. Why these ingredients were supposed to gain all their effectiveness from being in this form, rather than in their natural form, remained a puzzle to me – as I should have thought the exact reverse would have been the case.

I bought a box at once, and was much interested in a statement I found therein, giving the different uses to which the tablets might be put, and the precise time, in each case, in which a complete cure might be confidently awaited. It began something like this:

| Pneumonia | 4 tablets | 2½ hours |
| General paralysis | 3 " | 2 " |
| Scarlet fever | 2 " | 1 " |
| Consumption | 4 " | 20 minutes |
| Cancer | 2 " | 15 " |
| Smallpox | 1 " | 5 " |
| Bronchitis | 1 " | 2 " |

and so on.

'You will notice the difference after the first dose,' Anne said to me, when I told her I had taken her advice and bought a box.

The reader will be struck by the remarkable fervour, combined with a passion for formal and precise scientific statement, which characterized this girl's speech when it came to advising me on medical matters. I myself was no longer struck by it, because I was already used to it. The truth was that Anne was the most frightful 'lecturer' when any matter of health was brought up, and I simply had to put up with it.

I do not mean that she was any different or worse in this respect than any other Moribundian pretty girl. In fact, the lovelier they were, the more seemingly created for frivolous pleasures alone, the more austere, admonitory, and pedantically accurate they insisted on being in all matters of this kind.

I did not actually take those tablets, because, according to my habit, I completely forgot to do so in the first few days after buying them, and, before I had a chance to remedy the matter, Anne was seized by another idea, which arose from an offer I made her.

It must be understood that (during the periods when she was not lecturing me) I was deeply in love with Anne, and I had begun to wonder whether some form of sexual repression was at the root of my trouble.

Marriage, of course, was out of the question, in view of my impending return and of the circumstances generally: and I still did not know in what way she would respond to any other suggestion. At last, however, I summoned up the courage (having taken the precaution of presenting her with a large box of 'Siljoy' stockings beforehand) to tell her that I was ill with longing for her and to ask her point-blank whether she would go away with me somewhere – to the seaside, perhaps, where no one would know anything about it.

Her reception of this offer was decidedly curious. She completely ignored the moral in favour of the medical aspect of the question. She said that I had reminded her of a fact which had completely eluded her, and which would completely account for my condition – in other words, she began lecturing me again.

'Of course!' she said. 'Why did I not think of it before? There comes a time in everyone's life when the doctor can help us no more, when mere "medicine" is of no avail. We are thoroughly "run down" and the only remedy open to us is a complete change – an entire novelty of atmosphere in entirely new surroundings. We have become "stale" in every way, and only the stimulus of new scenery and new people will "put us to rights". Relaxation and rest is what we require, and "Dame Nature" will do the rest.'

This, so far, was hopeful but non-committal, and I waited eagerly for what she was going to say next.

'For this purpose,' she went on, 'what more ideal spot could be found than warm, sunny Seabrightstone? There, if you wish to be utterly idle, you may lounge, full-length, upon the golden, gleaming sands all day, building "castles in the air" with no one to say nay. Seabrightstone boasts some of the finest hotels in the country, and all doctors are agreed that its climate is unrivalled anywhere. Come to sunny Seabrightstone, and know what it is to feel "on top of the world" again!'

Her use of the word 'come' instead of the word 'go' at the end of this odd speech enabled me to take the whole as warm acquiescence in my proposal. I embraced her rapturously and asked her how soon she would be ready to begin the journey.

She said that she could manage it in a day or two, and seemed quite unaware of the thrilling implications of her acceptance. But, actually, it was I who did not know what I was letting myself in for, as we shall see.

We set off together three days later, taking a train which brought us into Seabrightstone in three hours. My spirits had risen temporarily and I enjoyed the journey down a great deal.

Seabrightstone was all that Anne had prophesied, and we put up at a hotel (quite as fine as the 'Moribundian') as man and wife.

At this stage, with apparently everything I could ask for on Moribundia, my cure should have been complete: but that is not what happened.

Of course, in a Moribundian seaside town the sun never ceases shining, and we bathed and lounged on the sands as we had planned. But instead of revelling in all this, my perverse worldly spirit, a thing which apparently can only take its pleasures relatively, which cannot understand freedom save as something identical with necessity itself, began again to rebel against these perfect conditions. I found myself yearning for a grey day and a fall of rain such as we have in England, and which I knew would never come.

But this was only part of my trouble. My relationship with Anne (sweet as she was attempting to be) grew more and more strained, and at last became intolerable.

As she was now freed from any of the exigencies of town life, it seemed that she had absolutely nothing else to think about but problems of physical health and beauty, and she was lecturing me every minute of the day. I simply could not stop her. Whatever we saw, whatever we did, wherever we went, she used as an occasion for delivering a sermon of some sort.

I had, for instance, only to say it was getting a little colder, and suggest I should fetch her coat, for her to begin: 'To stand up against the weather is not to go about loaded with mackintosh, coat, and umbrella – it is rather to be warmed, protected, invigorated from *within*. For this purpose Flakewheat contains all those body-building and nutritive properties which are absorbed so rapidly into the system that ..., etc., etc.' I never listened to the end of these talks.

Or, if I quite casually remarked that a light under which we were sitting was a little too strong, I would get: 'Yes, under the merciless glare of modern lighting conditions, which shows up every flaw of the skin, a girl's choice of make-up becomes a matter of paramount importance. Intensive research in the Laboratories extending over twelve years has now shown that 'Powdrall' alone contains the properties necessary ..., etc., etc.'

Or, if I happened to call her attention to a little boy on the beach who had dirtied himself by falling into a puddle, I would get: 'Yes – but it would be hardly human to scold the energetic little chappy. No doubt, even at that age, his mother has inculcated in him the healthful 'Savelife Soap' habit, which he will keep to the end of his days. Let him play as he wishes. His mother knows that all danger of germs and dirt contamination is ... etc., etc.'

Even if I asked her to pass the mustard at a meal, she would reply: 'Certainly, in addition to setting the salivary juices in action at once, and so stimulating the primary stages of digestion, mustard, by breaking down rich, indigestible fats, and breaking up the long fibres of lean, makes the task of assimilation … etc., etc.'

But this sort of thing was only a part of what I had to suffer. It must be understood that Anne prided herself upon being a 'modern' or 'up-to-date' Moribundian woman, and no one on earth could realize what this entails for anyone living on intimate terms with one of them.

'In the rush and general "tempo" of modern life,' Anne once said to me, 'no woman, if she requires to be smart, can possibly afford to neglect the smallest detail which will help to further beautify her, or give her that added appearance of "chic".'

To give a detailed description of what the adherence to these principles involved in, say, the simple act of going to bed and to sleep alone, is a task almost beyond me.

That she should have washed or had a bath, cleaned her teeth, brushed her hair, and applied some cream to her face, would have been nothing more than I could have expected. Nor did she disappoint me in these respects. Unfortunately, however, 'no modern woman could possibly risk personal freshness and daintiness' by neglecting the practice of daily dipping her underclothes in a certain preparation, and she was quite ten minutes in the bathroom doing this. I would keep on calling to her, and she would at last come out, only to retire a moment later, with an eye-bath. 'Every modern woman,' she said, 'knows the value of clean, sparkling eyes, and the extreme danger of neglecting them.'

I did not believe that she could take more than five minutes bathing her eyes, and so, after she had been in there for at least half an hour, I would call out to her again in exasperation. She would reply, in a preoccupied way, that 'nothing was so disfiguring as unsightly superfluous hair', and that as 'scientific research had at last found a method which would, by a little daily attention, painlessly remove even the most stubborn growth', that was what she was doing now.

Finally she would come out, and I would foolishly delude myself by thinking that she was at last coming to bed. Instead of this, however, there would be a lecture on the value 'for health and beauty alike' of 'scrupulous inner cleanliness', and she would begin taking laxatives and salts.

This would be followed by a long 'treatment' to counteract what she called 'the danger of excessive fat, imposing a terrible strain on the heart and other organs', and by another treatment morbidly undertaken to combat any tendency 'to dandruff or falling hair', the lotion which she massaged into her head being, she told me, 'the result of a wonderful piece of research by a famous bio-chemist, and recommended by hundreds of hair specialists all over Moribundia'.

Then there would be a sort of half-time interval in which she would stand in her underclothes gazing for hours (or it seemed hours to me) in an inquiring way at some undissolved soap in a tumblerful of water.

It goes without saying that Anne would not dream of retiring to bed without her nightly cup of 'Nourishine', without which, she told me, her dietary would lack the essential mineral salts, vitamins, calcium and iron required to sustain and energize the whole nervous system. And, of course, every night she indulged in a facial massage, with a carefully-chosen preparation to 'bring new life to the delicate tissues of the skin'.

This, of course, was not the only cream she was compelled to use. There were dozens. There was one specially created for 'glamour', one to 'counteract external acidity', one to 'wake up the underpores', one to supply 'the essential skin vitamins'. And so on and so forth.

I have still said nothing of the eye-lash growers, the cuticle removers, the nail polishes, the deodorants, the powders, the scents, etc. – the regular daily use of all of which, every twenty-four hours, if she really considered her health and beauty, no Moribundian woman could possibly afford to neglect.

Some feeble idea will, I hope, by now have been given of the time it took Anne to get to bed, and it will be understood why, when at last she was ready, looking most repulsive in her sleeping helmet, her skin-softening gloves, her chin-moulder, her nose-corrector and shoulder support, I myself was bored to extinction by her and generally fast asleep. There can be no doubt that it was in view of these conditions and circumstances that she had so readily consented to come away with me in the first place.

# CHAPTER TWELVE

In addition to the general despondency and gloom which lay upon my spirit at this time, and which no form of Moribundian treatment could dispel, I was now visited by a fresh torment from quite a different quarter. It was undoubtedly at this period (and since my return I have checked the dates carefully) that Crowmarsh began to make certain minute adjustments to his machine, or, as I would say, he began fiddling about with it, in much the same way as an over-zealous owner of a wireless might lightly touch the knobs, in order to extract greater clarity or volume, in the middle of a concert from Queen's Hall. No doubt this furnished him with various reassurances of a subtle technical nature, but to me the experience was utterly and stupendously terrifying.

The first time that this happened was one morning when Anne and I were lying on the beach at Seabrightstone. We had recentiy bathed, and were both lying flat looking up into the sky.

I do not know whether the reader has ever, at any time, suffered from what is with some people an avowed ailment, fear of heights. A lot of people will admit that in certain circumstances they have had intimations of this terror, while others will say that they are chronically afraid of heights of any sort. I have good reason, now, to believe that neither class has any notion of what it is talking about. For people to say that they are afraid of heights, and yet to lie, as they all do at the seaside, flat down on this little ball of ours, the Earth, and gaze coolly, impudently, one might say calculatingly, up into the infinite height of the sky above them, is to me the most absurd of contradictions. It is to me quite plain that one of the most remarkable attributes of the human organism as a whole is just this – that it is most miraculously constructed *not* to be afraid of heights – not even infinite ones.

I thought, however, as everyone else did until that day on the sands at Seabrightstone, when Crowmarsh began to play with his *Asteradio*. I was looking up into the blue sky, thinking of nothing in particular, when I slowly became conscious of a sort of whirring sound in my ears, combined with a sensation almost impossible to describe in words. It seemed that mentally I was drawn up to a fixed point, say, at a rough estimate, about seventy thousand billion billion miles away in the blue space above me, while my tiny body (tiny in comparison with the distance I had mentally travelled) remained most horribly where it was. Please remember, unmoved reader, perhaps at this very moment lying on the sands with this book, that there *is* an actually existing point about seventy thousand billion billion miles away from you in the space above you. Such a thing is not an imaginative fiction.

I can say very little more about this, my first sensation. Many people have stood directly underneath a New York sky-scraper and been terrified, on looking up, by their own smallness in relation to the cliff above them. Well, try to conceive the mental sky-scraper which towered above me at that moment, upon whose vast side my little body was stuck, and think how giddy I was. This, however, was something quite mild in comparison with the experience which immediately followed. In conjunction with my loss of all sense of normal size, there came a loss of all sense of gravity or direction, such as I pray I may never know again.

Columbus, you will remember, was discouraged from going to the other side of a world which he believed to be a round world, on the argument of the sheer absurdity of such a proposition. If the world was round, it was said, then, on the other side, the trees and flowers were growing upside down, human beings were standing, or walking about, on their heads, houses were built downwards, clouds were floating about beneath them, and when it rained it would have to rain upwards against the roofs. Nor has this argument ever been gainsaid. If anyone in England is going to presume that he is, as he feels he knows he is, the 'right way up', then he has, at the same time, to admit that, at the moment of his making that mental assumption, the people in Australia must be the 'wrong way up', standing on their heads. The same thing applies to anyone in Australia, making the same mental assumption in regard to the English. What is noticeable is that members of neither side will admit to standing on their heads, and English people and Australians are subconsciously calling each other liars with every breath they take and every act they perform. The double fiction, or the double truth, serves us well, however, and keeps us all sane. But imagine the plight of someone who momentarily loses his faculty for belief in the requisite fiction, who can only visualize the reverse fiction, who can only see himself hanging and looking downwards into the infinite abyss of space, his feet somehow stuck, like a fly's, to the vast stretch and weight of an earth now sweeping away in all directions and in all its multiformity *above* him!

That is what I now felt. I sprang to my feet. The blood came surging into my head. Gravity, I felt, could no longer hold me.

In another moment I would go plunging off into the blue abyss beneath me. I was not on top of the earth, the whole earth was on top of me!

I could see, just above me, and near to me, Anne, asleep in the sun and herself stuck by some accountable attraction to the sand from which she, too, must in the next second fly off with me into space!

I called to her, I wanted to cling to her, to save myself from going. She took no notice – she, and the whole earth, were on top of me and against me! My heart was thumping, my ear were singing. I flung out my arms and screamed. I saw her eyes open; I saw her stare down at me in terror, and bewilderedly reach her arms down towards me: I tried to reach up to her, but could not do so and screamed again. I found myself struggling in her arms, and everything went dark. Merciful universe, in which all, at last, goes dark! When I came round, a few minutes later, the sky was above me again, and I was lying on, not under, a familiar looking world, in a state of confusion as to what exactly had happened.

It is easy enough to see how this looked to Anne, who had been lying beside me. I must have seemed suddenly to have sprung from my sleep in the sun, to have made awful epileptic movements above her, and then fallen upon her in a swoon – the whole performance resembling a seizure, or heart attack, or nightmare of some sort. When she questioned me about it, indeed, I said that I had had a nightmare, and left it at that, as I could never have explained the truth to her, and I was terrified of dwelling on the subject lest that awful angle of vision might return.

There can be no doubt that these subjective sensations were produced objectively by Crowmarsh's fiddling with the

*Asteradio* – by the fact that he was somehow tentatively 'pulling' at me, dragging me away from the planet Moribundia experimentally or in preparation for my ultimate return. The reader will now have some intimation, I hope, of what it feels like, to be hauled off one world in the direction of another! The knobs having been adjusted, in merciless disregard for any feelings I might have, the concert went on.

This first one was the worst attack of its kind which I was made to endure, but by no means the last. Thereafter it seemed that Crowmarsh had a fit of asteradial 'nerves', and almost daily I was made conscious of the fact by sensations similar to those described above. They might come upon me anywhere and at any time – on the sands, at the hotel, in the streets, during a meal, while taking a bath. I was now pretty sure what was happening, however, and my terror was somewhat modified both by this knowledge and by the similarity, and at last familiarity, of the sensations themselves. Indeed, I believe a time might have come when I could have faced and endured the feeling of hanging upside down in eternity almost with no other emotion than one of curiosity – of relish even, of its excessive novelty!

But, of course, it was only after much suffering that I felt the approach of any such feeling of immunity, and I cannot exaggerate the miserable state of incessant apprehensiveness and fright I was in at this period.

Above all, there was the awful thought, which I tried to fight down, that 'something had gone wrong' up there (I thought of our world now as 'up there') and that I should never get back. Certain travellers on the sea complain of a subdued feeling of uncertainty and fright when half-way out on a long voyage. Imagine the feelings of one who is half-way out on a journey through the sea of space and senses the fact that the engines are behaving in a dubious and hesitant manner! And, instead of 'seasickness', think of those height-sensations of mine as a form of 'world-sickness', the sickening sense of the motion of the waves being replaced by the sickening sense of the motion of planets!

I should have said that these attacks did not begin to take place until I had been about two weeks at Seabrightstone. Among other things, they had the effect of reminding me in a forcible manner that the period allotted to my stay in Moribundia was by no means limitless. 'About three months,' Crowmarsh had said, and I now awoke to the fact that two of those months would very soon have gone. At the same time I realized that there was a tremendous amount more to be seen and done if I was to bring back anything resembling a complete account or summary of this strange world, and I began to chafe to get back to *Nwotsemaht*.

However, I was persuaded by Anne to stay on another ten days, and I filled in the time by consuming an enormous amount of Moribundian literature, about which I will have something to say later. Then the day came when we took a train back.

Anne returned to her house in town with her father, and I went back to the 'Moribundian.'

Here I was given the warmest and most flattering reception by the clerk, upon whose countenance there remained not a trace of that haggard illness and worry for which I had learned to look. Instead he was smiling broadly, bustling about like mad, and showing wonderful efficiency. In spite of a heavy rush of business he not only remembered my name, he remembered the number of my old room and each of my personal requirements, and was the soul of bright and brimming courtesy.

As I left the desk I happened to see the manager come out to have a word, or rather balloon, with him. This is what it was:

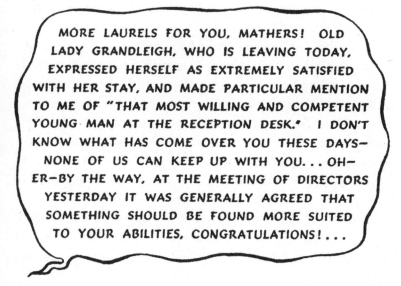

MORE LAURELS FOR YOU, MATHERS!  OLD LADY GRANDLEIGH, WHO IS LEAVING TODAY, EXPRESSED HERSELF AS EXTREMELY SATISFIED WITH HER STAY, AND MADE PARTICULAR MENTION TO ME OF "THAT MOST WILLING AND COMPETENT YOUNG MAN AT THE RECEPTION DESK."  I DON'T KNOW WHAT HAS COME OVER YOU THESE DAYS—NONE OF US CAN KEEP UP WITH YOU... OH—ER—BY THE WAY, AT THE MEETING OF DIRECTORS YESTERDAY IT WAS GENERALLY AGREED THAT SOMETHING SHOULD BE FOUND MORE SUITED TO YOUR ABILITIES, CONGRATULATIONS!...

To which the clerk gratefully and modestly threw back on the air:

THANK YOU SIR!
AFTER ALL, I ONLY TRY TO DO MY BEST.
THE HOTEL COMES FIRST.

adroitiy head-ballooning at the same time:

THINKS.
I OWE THIS ADVANCEMENT TO "NOURISHINE".

The day after this the clerk disappeared from the desk, and I never saw him again.

Presumably he had gone on to better things.

It was good to be back in the capital again, and in the next few days I found my spirits reviving a little. We had a little rain, and cold, and fog, all of which put new life into me, though it set the Moribundians coughing and sneezing, and rushing to their remedies – and, with my return from Seabrightstone, Crowmarsh made no further onslaughts upon my position in space. You could have imagined that he had somehow sensed and disapproved of my idling down there by the seaside!

But in the remainder of my stay in Moribundia I was not fated ever to know again my first contentment. My next trouble and problem broke out from the least expected quarter – from Anne herself, in fact.

# CHAPTER THIRTEEN

I do not know exactly when I first began to notice it, but it was not long after our return to town that the suspicion broke upon my mind that Anne was avoiding me.

I cannot pretend that I had been remarkably lover-like during the latter part of our stay – indeed, I had felt that a little rest from each other would do neither of us any harm; and though we had met for dinner one night I had not made any special effort to see her during the first few days after we got back.

She began, I think, by being evasive over the 'phone, either leaving it to her maid to answer, or, when it was impossible to do this, pleading other engagements or business when I suggested a meeting. I took little notice of this at first, but at last it became so obvious that, still pretending that nothing was the matter, I began to set little telephonic traps for her, and positively forced her – if she was to save her face – to make an appointment with me. Under this kind of pressure, she did arrange to meet me, though only for half an hour for a drink, and though I could see she was trying hard to behave with me as usual, it was equally clear that something was wrong.

Not wishing to appear too anxious, I still ignored this strange behaviour on her part, and got her to agree to meet me the next day. Her maid telephoned to break this appointment, and in the next three days I was unable to establish any contact with her at all.

I decided that she must have grown tired of me, and in a fit of *pique* reminded myself that 'there were plenty of other fish in the sea'. Moribundia, as I have made clear, was brimming over with beautiful girls, plenty of whom were staying at the hotel, and I now had quite enough confidence in myself to open an acquaint-anceship with any one of them.

I actually did make the acquaintance of several such girls. I noticed, though, that after my first few conversations or meetings with them, they all began to behave in very much the same way as Anne was behaving, that is to say, avoiding me politely, but like the plague.

Before long I was altogether disquieted, and 'phoned up Anne again in desperation. As I had anticipated, I was not allowed to speak to her, but I was not going to let this stand in my way. Going out and buying a large box of 'Siljoy' stockings (in whose efficacy for such a situation as this I had every reason to believe), I walked round to the street in which she lived and waited in the region of her house until she came out.

She came out in due course, and I must say looked extremely startled and guilty when I stepped up to her. For a moment I thought she was going to be angry, but when her eye fell upon the box of stockings under my arm, a strange, sad, half-longing, half-pitying look came into her eyes. I could see that she was undergoing some extraordinary inner conflict – that she was being torn between two feelings.

At any rate she consented to walk along with me, and I at once plied her with questions.

'Why are you avoiding me, Anne?' I asked. 'What has come over you? What is the matter with me?'

At this she murmured something I could not hear, and she refused to meet my eyes.

'But you must tell me,' I said. 'Surely you will let me know what is the matter with me. I am alone in this world – I have told you all about myself – I always thought you were my best friend here. What is wrong? Are you not my best friend?'

'Yes,' she said, 'that's just it.'

'What do you mean? If you are my best friend, surely you can tell me what is the matter?'

'You don't understand . . . ' she said.

'Then it comes to this,' I said. 'Even my best friend won't tell me? Is that it?'

'Yes,' she said, looking at me in an extraordinary way. 'That's exactly it.'

I was so angry at this that I thrust the box of 'Siljoy' stockings into her hands, and, with a curt 'Good-bye, then', walked away.

My rage lasted some time, but its exhilaration passed away only too soon and left me with a feeling of despondency and loneliness which grew worse and worse as the day declined and the evening drew on, and became at last unbearable.

I tried to enter into conversation with several odd people, or even groups of people, at the hotel, but it seemed in each case that after a few minutes they made some excuse to go away and leave me alone.

Finally I became so wretched that I foolishly decided to take the only form of escape now open to me, that is, to get drunk.

Before doing this, however, I took the precaution of first of all going upstairs and changing into evening clothes. I was instinctively aware that no one, no male at any rate (and women, apart from charwomen, never get drunk in Moribundia), was ever seen in this condition on the streets save in evening clothes and top hat, and, already suspecting that I must have unconsciously sinned against some obscure Moribundian canon, I was not going consciously and openly to defy any convention.

I certainly got drunk that night, but I should here explain that Moribundian alcohol has an effect upon the brain and nervous system quite different from anything we know on earth.

After only a few drinks, for instance, I found my speech suffering from the most unnatural impediment or addition, which took the form of my being compelled to interpolate, after every three or four words, a word which I at once realized was either the Latin word for 'this', or the American word for country bumpkin – that is to say 'hic', or 'hick'. This continued throughout the entire evening, and, in addition to betraying my condition to every observer, must have sounded ineffably absurd.

In addition to this I found myself converting almost every available consonant into the 'sh' sound.

Thus, when after several drinks in the hotel bar, I was asking the hotel porter the way out into the street, instead of simply saying: 'I say, porter, is this the way out into the street?' I found myself addressing him thus:

'I shay – hic – portersh – hic – ish thish – hic – the waysh out – hic – intosh shtreet – hic?'

But such disorders of the speech are merely the preliminary effects which the Moribundian alcohol has upon the system. Very soon afterwards I found that my nose was going a deep beetroot red colour: I had completely lost my balance on my feet, my tie was undone, my top hat was battered, and I was making the most fantastic errors of judgment and vision. For instance, I was constantly under the impression that I saw two, or even three, people, when only one was standing before me! Thus, in speaking to anyone, I was always making reference to 'both of you' or 'your twin brother' or 'the middle one', and causing the greatest amusement to those who watched me.

Towards the close of the evening I met several other people

who were in the same state, and with whom, from time to
time, I formed a sort of bewildered alliance. It is the instinct
of the Moribundian drunk man to seek a companion in a similar condition, upon whose arm he may hang, and to whom
he may make his fatuous observations without rebuff; and, of
course, one drunk man can recognize another instantly by his
evening dress and general appearance. At one time, indeed,
as many as five of us joined together, and, arm-in-arm, sang
in chorus an old sentimental Moribundian song called *Teews
Enileda* – this with great feeling, but, of course, hopelessly
out of tune.

All these other drunk people were behaving in just the same
way as myself and making the same absurd mistakes – that is
to say, imagining that animal hearth-rugs were genuine jungle
beasts, that statues of women were alive and admonishing or
inviting them, that area-railings were the bars of a prison, that
they were engaged in long-distance swimming when they had
in reality only fallen into horses' drinking troughs, etc., etc.
Under the circumstances, and with all these delusions, snares
and pitfalls, the simple business of getting home assumed the
proportions of a Homeric journey, and I do not know how any
of us would have got back had there not been a lot of policemen
about – 'Conshtabalsh' as we called them – who in collaboration with a great number of milkmen pointed out our mistakes
to us, let us drape ourselves around them, and generally took
care of us.

Needless to say, I had the most indescribably awful 'head'
the next morning, which I tried to cure in the traditional
Moribundian manner, that is, by tying, or trying to tie, an enormous piece of ice on to the top of my head. But I felt so absolutely
beastly while this was on, and my neck and clothes got so wet,

that I soon abandoned it, reckoning that the remedy was worse than the ailment.

My depression that morning knew no bounds. Not only was I feeling sick, not only was everybody shunning me, not only was I thoroughly ashamed of myself for having made such a fool of myself the night before: another problem had arisen from the fact that the usual amount of money which appeared in my pocket daily from nowhere – twenty-five pounds – had suddenly been reduced to the meagre sum of five pounds only. I had noticed that this had been happening for two or three days previously, and I had imagined that some mistake had been made and the matter would right itself: it now became apparent that hence forward this was to be my income.

To this day I do not quite understand the cause of this sudden drop. I can only surmise that as in Moribundia the amount of a man's income was in direct proportion to his merit some loss of merit on my part was being reflected in this way. Perhaps it was the immorality of having taken Anne away to the seaside; perhaps it was my extreme laziness while I was there; perhaps it was this social crime which I seemed to have committed, which caused people to shun me, but about which they would tell me nothing. Whatever the cause, there it was, and I realized with the acutest displeasure that at this rate I should not be able to go on staying at the 'Moribundian'. I had been ordering everything I wanted, and I owed them a large bill already.

I even feared that if this went on I might be obliged to acquire the requisite amount of merit by doing some sort of work. Such a fate, with the disastrous result it would have of curtailing to a minimum the remaining time at my disposal for scientific investigation, had to be avoided at all costs. You will notice that I had by now abandoned any project I ever had of trying to explain who and what I was to the authorities, and getting public support from them. I knew by now that if I did so I would be regarded as a lunatic, and probably locked up. However inadequately I have portrayed Moribundia so far, I think I have at least made it clear that the one thought the Moribundian, by his nature, is incapable of entertaining, is the thought that there may be any conceivable world of things and ideas other than his own. Merely to mention, let alone to propound, such a theory in public, would be to be regarded as a madman, or worse perhaps, a *Tsixram*.

I was, then, with one thing and another, worried almost to the point of desperation. It soon became quite clear that I would have to clear out of the 'Moribundian' and take up my abode in some more humble place. It was this last realization which at last gave me the solution to my troubles.

It dawned upon me, in a flash, that my life on this planet up to this moment had been spent exclusively amongst the upper and middle classes, and that apart from a few bus-conductors and *Yenkcocs* I had seen nothing of the lower orders and poor as a whole, the labouring classes, the toilers in their own surroundings.

It was clear that, from the point of view of social investigation, I could not possibly overlook this side of Moribundian life. Why not then, since I was seemingly being shunned and cold-shouldered by everyone in this present station of life, go and live amongst the working people, whom I might not offend, and who might accord me more simple and human treatment? At the same time I could study their habits at first hand, and certainly gain a less one-sided view of Moribundian society.

Also, I would not be living above my income. As soon as I came to these conclusions I felt an enormous measure of relief, and decided to act upon them without delay. I still had enough money to pay my bill at the 'Moribundian', and I did so at once. Then, with only three pounds in my pocket and a suitcase containing a few clothes and necessities, I stepped out into the street, and boarded a bus in the direction of the working-class districts, which lie to the east of *Nwotsemaht*.

# CHAPTER FOURTEEN

I dismounted from the bus at a point at which, so I had been told, the homes of the working people began, but I could not believe at first that I had reached my destination. This was because the working-class districts in Moribundia are so entirely different from anything we know on our own earth.

There were, it is true, several humble grey dwellings of the type which I had expected to see, but these were so completely hidden away and absorbed by the other features, that I at first could hardly realize the fact that they were there at all.

My first impression was, indeed, that instead of being in the working-class district I had alighted upon some strange, rather sordid sort of Coney Island on its outskirts – a neighbourhood entirely devoted, not to work, but to amusement. Nearly every other building, it seemed to me, was either a cinema or a place of entertainment, and I have never seen so many cars, so many greyhounds, so many fur coats, so many silk stockings and so many idle people bent on pleasure in my life. But it was the number of the cinemas which impressed me most.

Surprised as I was, I regained my composure when I recollected certain facts in the history of the Moribundian working class, facts with which I was then acquainted, but about which the reader will, of course, know nothing.

There was, it seems, a time when the working people suffered very considerably from bad housing conditions, insecurity, overwork and penury. But now all that has been changed. In very much the same way that 'modern' science completely replaced and eliminated 'old-fashioned' science in Moribundia, so 'modern conditions' have replaced the 'old conditions', and the 'present-day' working man has replaced the old-fashioned one.

Whereas the old-fashioned working man led a life of toil and received very little in return, the modern working man does practically nothing, and as any Moribundian authority will tell you, 'has everything'.

His income is admittedly not so large as that of his social superior, but this is 'made up for him' in so many ways that it would be difficult to say that he is not a great deal better off materially. In fact, nearly everything which other people have to buy with money, is to him either given freely or is so cheap that it can scarcely be said to touch his pocket at all. If I began to make a list of his assets – if I began to speak of the free hospitals, the free libraries, the free schools, the free insurance – or the cheap wireless, the cheap cars, the cheap clothes, the cheap cinemas and entertainments, etc. – I should not know where to stop.

How far the Moribundian working man is 'grateful' for these Moribundian advantages, the use to which he puts them, and the effect they have upon his character, are different matters which I will come to later when I describe the working-class family with which I stayed.

As I have said, in addition to the cinemas and places of amuse-ment, there still remained a few dwellings of the type, more or less, which I expected to see, and it was amongst these that I wandered, looking for somewhere where I might lodge.

I had to wander a long way before I could find anything, but at last I came across a house with a board in the window saying 'Room to Let', and, with a feeling of relief, I put down the bag on the step and rang the bell.

My ring was not immediately answered, but as there was a wireless blaring away at full blast inside the house, and as there were other wirelesses blaring away at full blast in all the other houses down the street, I was not surprised at this, and rang again more loudly. This still had no effect, and so I was compelled to use the knocker violently. At last I heard someone coming, and the door was opened by a young man with such a rude manner, and of so untidy and slouching an appearance, that I felt I wanted to shake him.

This, I later learned, was the son of the house, Bill Juggins. At his heels there were two very well-kept but rather over-fed bulldogs.

With all the politeness I could muster I asked him if I could see the room which was advertised in the window, but he said that he knew nothing about it, and that I would have to ask his mother about it.

I asked him if I could see his mother, but he said she was out. She was at the cinema. Also he himself was just leaving for a football match. I could, however, if I wished, wait inside until his mother returned.

I accepted his offer and he conducted me into a living-room on the right of the passage. Here there was a small child with a hopelessly untended appearance, and who looked to me as though it was underfed. The young man took no notice of this child, but before he went out, I noticed, he went to a large refrigerator which stood in one corner of the room and took out two enormous lumps of prime beef steak (each weighing at least five pounds) and threw then to the bulldogs, who ate them on an expensive Turkish rug, in front of the fire. I need hardly add that before going out he made no attempt to save the current by turning off the wireless.

It was still early in the afternoon, and I had to wait something like two hours before his mother returned. But at last she came in, and I was pleased to find that she had a much more prepossessing appearance and character than her son.

Mrs Juggins, in point of fact, was a more or less old-fashioned soul, a Mary Brough-like type of the old school, who could still vividly remember the days before the great revolution in working-class conditions of which I have spoken, and who had not even yet fully adjusted her mind and habits to the wonderful change.

She greeted me most hospitably and apologized for having kept me waiting so long – for having been, indeed, out of doors when I arrived.

'But there you are,' she said. 'That's what life is for us workin' women of to-day. With all these modern conveniences – what with cheap electricity, cheap vacuum cleaners, running hot and cold water, and all the other innumerable devices for relieving the burden of domestic tasks, each within the reach of the humblest purse – the modern housewife can do in as many minutes what used to take hours. The word drudgery can no longer be applied to domestic work. Why, look at to-day. Everything was finished in a quarter of an hour, and by nine o'clock I was free to go out for a spin in the new car with my old man. Then I went on to the cinema, where I saw as fine a show as you could see anywhere for a few pence – and here I am.'

'Remarkable,' I said. 'You must feel the change enormously.'

'Oh, yes, it's nice enough,' she replied, 'but bless your heart, do we appreciate it? Are we thankful for it? Of course not. Instead of being grateful for what we've got, all we do is to ask for more. And it all comes out of the tax-payers' money too.'

I should here explain that in Moribundia the working classes are exempt from any form of taxation, direct or indirect, and that almost the entire bulk of the tax-payers' money is given over to the furnishing of the working class with these luxuries.

I now asked her if I could see the room she had to let, and she took me upstairs. The room was pleasant enough, and the sheets on the bed looked to me immaculately clean. It was not clean enough for this excellent soul, however. She said, indeed, looking at me in a rather shocked way, that she thought her linen was white until she saw it next to my newly-washed handkerchief, and she added that she would have it changed before I slept in the bed.

We then went downstairs again, where, with the aid of an electric kettle and grilling device, tea and toast were made in less than a minute. After this we had a talk, and as the evening drew on we were joined by the youngest daughter of the house, Mary, who had returned from her work.

She was, physically, a most attractive young thing, expensively, if somewhat flashily, dressed, and she had an indolent, pampered and haughty air which confirmed my impression that the children of this household, having been brought up under the new conditions, were certainly not the equal of their mother in character and courtesy. This girl, I soon discovered, worked as a domestic servant.

'You're home very early, Mary,' said her mother. 'Got the evening off?'

'Oh, no,' said Mary, in the most matter-of-fact tone. 'I walked out of the place, and gave her a piece of my mind, too.'

'Dear me,' said her mother, but she scarcely seemed surprised. 'That's the fourth situation you've left this week. What was the trouble this time?'

'Of all the blooming cheek,' said Mary, 'she complained when I gave a cocktail party to a few friends in the kitchen, and then asked me if I'd occasionally do the washing up after lunch!'

This took even her mother aback, in spite of her old-fashioned principles, and she said: 'Well, well, I'm not surprised you left.'

If this should cause wonderment or astonishment in the reader (as no doubt it will) he should understand that in Moribundia the relations between maid and mistress, as we know them, are entirely reversed and distorted. Up there it is nothing for a mistress literally (and when I say literally, I mean literally) to go down on her knees to beg a maid or a cook to stay with her; and this absolute slavishness on one side is manifested in all their dealings with each other. It is nothing for a mistress to implore, to entreat, to bribe by any means her servant to perform so simple an act of grace as staying on to cook a meal in the evening; and employers will go about in a state of incessant, miserable nervousness and trepidation lest a tactless word should be uttered and heard in the kitchen. Cook-generals in particular are appallingly tyrannical, and, it seems to me, consciously cruel under these conditions, having an awful way of folding their arms, and frowning in a basilisk stare, which puts such terror into the hearts of their supposed superiors that they visibly tremble and quake before them, stuttering their apologies. It is a wonder to me that these servants are ever employed at all, since I myself would put up with any sort of hardship rather than suffer such snubbing and humiliation. On the other hand, it is a wonder that they themselves, being in such a strong position, ever condescend to go into service, if service it can be called.

'These mistresses are above themselves these days,' Mary went on. 'And she was only giving me five pounds a week, too!'

I knew too much of Moribundia now to do anything other than acquiesce in the ideas I found prevalent therein, and I joined with Mary's mother in applauding the sentiments which had led her to walk haughtily out of a situation in which she had been so scandalously treated.

Soon afterwards we were joined by Bill, the son of the house, who had returned from his football match. It soon became apparent that this young man was out of work – had been out of work for months in fact, and was living on the dole.

The most extraordinary conversation, but one utterly characteristic of the younger working-class man, now followed. His mother asked him whether he had been to the Labour Exchange that day, to see if anything had turned up that he could do.

'Oh, yes,' he answered morosely, 'I went along.'

'Was there nothing for you?' asked his mother.

'Oh, yes,' he said, 'there were plenty of jobs. They're crying for men. They always are.'

'What was the matter, then?' asked his mother. 'Weren't they the sort of jobs you could do?'

'Do them?' he replied in the same gloomy way. 'Of course I could. But catch *me*.'

I think he must have seen that I looked a little surprised at this, for he added, looking at me:

'Why should I, when I can live on the tax-payers' money?'

His mother and sister quietly nodded at this, as though it were axiomatic, and the subject was dropped, but personally I began to feel that I had come to live in a sort of madhouse.

At about six o'clock we were joined by the father of the family, Mr Juggins, who had finished his work for the day.

When I say we were joined by him, I do not want to give the impression that I had not seen him before; for he had, as a matter of fact, been coming into the house and going out of it again at short intervals ever since four o'clock. He was, as it happened, a plumber by trade, and was working on a job at a house not far away. The trouble with this man was that he was absolutely incapable of remembering to take the necessary tools with him, and was always having to come back to fetch those he required.

This deficiency of memory amounted, in my eyes, to a positive mania, possibly sexual at root, and for which he might profitably have been treated by a psycho-analyst; but he and his family treated these exits and entrances in the most matter-of-fact way.

Frequently, instead of returning himself, he sent his 'mate' back to fetch the desired implement. Naturally, no work on the house could be started until the tools were assembled; and since, as I learned later, he charged at the fullest rate for the time spent merely in going to and fro, I could not help feeling a pang of pity for the householder who had called him in.

My impression, then, of being in a madhouse was increased rather than lessened by the behaviour of the father, but this was nothing compared with that of the last member of the family, who came in now – the eldest girl, Joan, who worked in a munition factory. At first she seemed normal enough, physically resembling her younger sister, Mary, though much more flashily dressed, and covered ostentatiously with jewels which I could see at once were genuine.

When she had come in the entire family was assembled in full force, and it was felt that it was an appropriate moment to prepare an evening meal.

They all joined in the task, and it pains me to describe the waste which took place on all sides. Joan, who earned an enormous salary at her factory, and who could literally afford to buy anything she wanted, had brought back with her the choicest foods of all kinds, and the extravagant way in which these were got ready was an agony to see. In the mere process of preparation alone, at least half of this expensive nourishment was thrown into the dustbin, or left to rot in the sink; the rest being cooked in villainously expensive butter, and finally being served, not on plates on a table with a table-cloth, but on the French polish of a beautiful grand piano, which stood in the sitting-room, and which Joan had lately purchased from her salary! Needless to say, when the meal was finished, so thoughtlessly had it been planned, that at least half of it was left over, and instead of being saved for the next day, it joined the rest of the refuse in the dustbin.

After 'dinner' Joan began to play, in an excruciatingly vulgar, crude and noisy way upon the piano; the others joined in with singing, and I did my best to bear it as well as I could.

In spite of their eccentricities they were all quite friendly towards myself personally – though I had to watch my p's and q's very carefully when addressing Mary, knowing that, from a habit of authority acquired in Moribundian domestic service, she might 'take offence' at the slightest thing.

When the singing and playing was over they all gathered round the fire, which was nearly out. It was this fact which caused what to me was the maddest and most distressing episode of the whole evening. For, instead of fetching coal, Joan walked out of the room and, returning a moment later with a chopper in her hand, proceeded methodically to hack away at her beautiful grand piano, gathering up the splinters and throwing them on the burning coals as firewood!

This was too much for me, and I begged her to desist, using the excuse that I would like to hear some more of her charming music. Flattered, I think, by this request, she willingly ceased to abuse the piano, but showed she had no inkling of my real meaning by at once picking up a beautiful old chair (a priceless antique for which she must have paid I know not what sum) and chopping it to pieces in front of my eyes.

Soon after this, warmed by the cheerful blaze of varnish and wood, I began to feel sleepy, and thought of going to bed. Seeing that this house had every other conceivable modern convenience, I presumed that there was a bathroom, and I asked Mrs Juggins whether I could have a bath before turning in.

She looked somewhat crestfallen at this, and said, doubtfully, that she would 'go and see'. She went out of the room, and returned almost immediately, saying that she was afraid I could not use the bath tonight, as the coal had been put into it, and it was full up.

'The coal!' I exclaimed.

'Yes,' she said. 'I'm sorry. That's where we keep the coal.'

I made light of the matter, but Mrs Juggins evidently felt that she was failing in her duties towards me as her guest. She suggested that one of the neighbours might have a bathroom which I could use. In spite of my protests she insisted that her son should go out with me and see if this was so, and if I could be accommodated.

I went out with Bill and we called next door. But here exactly the same thing happened. The coal had been put into the bath. We then called on the neighbour on the other side, but a summary inspection showed again that the bath had been put to the same extraordinary use. Not willing to be defeated, I think we called – in all – on about a dozen houses that night, all the way down the street, but in each case we met with a similar result.

We had to give in at last, which I was glad enough to do. I made my excuses and went to bed at once, falling into a deep sleep after an unexpectedly exhausting day.

# CHAPTER FIFTEEN

I see that in describing that afternoon and evening with the Juggins family I have given a summary, for all practical purposes, of their entire activities, from which they never varied for a single day or in a single direction. I had hoped that when I had been with them some time innumerable interesting conditions and customs would come to light, but I waited in vain.

Every day was monotonously the same. Every morning Mrs Juggins, having finished her housework in an incredibly short space of time, went off complacently to the cinema: at the same time the elder girl went to her factory, the younger to her latest mistress, and her brother to the Labour Exchange. Mr Juggins alone was visible in the middle of the day, being in and out all the time for the tools he had left behind. Then, in the evening, they all came in in the same order, and there was enacted a scene similar to the one I have given. Every other evening Mary had left her employment on account of some trifling infringement of the rules she laid down for her employers, and Bill, whilst still telling of the countless jobs open for him to take, continued to scorn the idea so long as he could live on the taxpayers' money.

The reader will have been able to judge for himself of the apathy, laziness, wilfulness and lack of initiative of this family, but it is not so easy to realize how depressing it is to live for any length of time amongst such people.

The trouble is that they are, and are acknowledged by all

Moribundians to be, quite 'hopeless'. There is nothing to be done about them.

Oddly enough, in a strange way they are themselves aware of their own defects. This was evidenced by a conversation I had with old Juggins one morning when he had come back for one of his tools. This, of course, was in the early part of my stay, when my reason and spirit still rebelled against the atrocities I was forced daily to witness.

Seeing that the old man was in a good mood and inclined to talk, I ventured to ask him if he did not think it would be better, if it would not make everybody a great deal happier, if he, to begin with, made some strenuous mental effort to remember his tools when he went to work, instead of wasting everybody's time by forgetting them and coming back for them in this foolish way. Similarly, I suggested that his youngest daughter might be a great deal more settled in her mind, and easier in her manner, if, by an effort of will, she could rid herself of this exasperated sensitiveness towards her employers: while I hinted that his eldest daughter would save a great deal of her money and a great deal of time and effort, if, instead of buying a new grand piano every week to be chopped up as firewood, she took the simple precaution of introducing a coal-scuttle into the sitting-room, and seeing, as a matter of daily routine, that the coal was put into it and not into the bath. Also, with reference to his son, I politely hinted that prolonged idleness could not be good for a young man, and I even threw doubt upon the ethical scrupulousness of living in this way upon the taxpayers' money.

He listened in a quiet and friendly way to what I had to say, but when I had finished he shook his head sadly and answered me.

'No,' he said. 'It's no good, there's nothing to be done about us. We're hopeless. We don't even try. Things aren't what they used to be. Why, in my grandfather's day a man was proud to do a job of work. He was conscientious. He took an interest in it. He respected his employer, and his employer respected him. He got a decent wage and did his best in return. But that's all changed. You don't get that nowadays. All we think of to-day is how we can *avoid* work – how we can *scamp* a job and get more money for it. There's not such a thing, any more, as honest pride in a job well done. We're thoroughly spoiled, that's what the matter is.

'Look at all these modern luxuries,' he went on, thoroughly warming to his argument. 'Look at the wireless, the cheap cinemas, the free insurance, the free holidays, the gas, the electricity, the equipment of all kinds. Compared with his old state the modern working man lives like a king in a palace. But do we appreciate it? Of course we don't. We don't even know how to make use of it. We don't *understand* beautiful things. If you give us a bathroom we only go and put the coal into it. If you give us beautiful furniture, we only go and break it up. You've seen for yourself. We're hopeless, that's what we are, plain hopeless, and there's nothing to be done about us.'

I was surprised at the old man's fatalism, his attitude of complete resignation towards the existing state of affairs, but I put it down to the fact that he was, after all, a Moribundian himself, and as such, like all other Moribundians, instinctively aware of the impossibility of any change.

The reader may by now have been thinking that I have contradicted myself over this matter of change – inasmuch as I have already taken pains to describe at least two major changes in Moribundia – two revolutions in fact – the revolution in 'Modern Science' and the revolution in 'Modern Conditions.' But the fault lies with Moribundia, not with me.

The most perplexing thing of all about Moribundia is that it willingly admits and knows change in the past, while absolutely denying it to the future.

This is simply the fact, and I can no more explain it than I can explain its balloons, its target-nosed women, or any other of its seeming contradictions of natural law.

The reader may, however, be permitted to ask how and why it has come about that, in an ideal, a perfect land, so useless, predatory and wasteful a class should be allowed to exist. This is a difficult question to answer, and my own theory is one that alludes again to this ever-present problem of change.

In my own view these people are allowed to exist as a sort of moral example, a visual and living proof of the danger and absurdity of making any radical change in the social system, of giving any further privileges to, or in any way trying to better the conditions of, the working people.

The reasonable Moribundian has only to observe the results of giving the working people what has been given them already, to see what fools and beasts they have made of themselves, and what worse fools and worse beasts they would undoubtedly make of themselves if they were given more. And so, although he knows his lesson well enough already, he has incessantly in front of his eyes a huge practical example of the disgusting results of change of any sort. To put it another way, this working class is, perhaps, a sort of homoeopathic serum injected into the body politic. But I should make it clear that this is only my surmise.

After only three or four days with the Juggins family I was tired of the monotony of their daily existence: after three or four weeks I was bored to distraction. In the long day that I had to myself, I did as much reading as I possibly could, and I went every day to one of the wonderful cinemas that abounded in the district. But nothing seemed to relieve the tedium, and I was looking back wistfully now on my life at the 'Moribundian' with Anne as on a paradise from which I had been expelled.

It seemed to be my fate in Moribundia not to know when I was well off, for after I had been about a month with the Juggins', something happened which made me look upon even my normal life with them as a perfectly happy and desirable mode of existence, and to long to have it given me again.

The blow fell with cruel suddenness one morning on waking in my little room.

Before I opened my eyes I was conscious of a feeling of fever, and an aching in my limbs, also a cramped sensation caused, I thought, through having remained in one position too long.

When I opened my eyes I saw the cause of this, and yet could hardly believe what I saw.

Over my pyjamas, wound sinuously around my torso and arms, binding me closely and painfully to the bed, were enormous chains, heavy as lead and at least two inches thick!

I instinctively and spontaneously struggled to escape, but could not move an inch.

I then realized that I must not get into a panic. I must think this thing out. Was this some preposterous practical joke which had been played upon me, or were the Juggins' a family of fiends, of *macabre* torturers of some sort? Who had done this to me?

At last I called out in a pathetic way, but no one answered me. Whereupon I let out such a yell of panic that both Mrs Juggins and her son, who were on the same landing, burst into my room at the same time.

'What *is* this?' I cried. 'What has happened to me? Have *you* done this?'

'Good heavens!' said Mrs Juggins to her son, after a pause in which she had looked at me with pity and dismay. 'He's chained to his bed by rheumatism!'

'What the devil do you mean?' I said, but they only continued to look at me.

'Yes,' said Bill ruefully at last. 'There's no doubt about what it is. He's chained to his bed by rheumatism.'

I then asked them if they would be good enough to unchain me instantly (rheumatism or not), but they only looked at me as though I were a madman, or speaking in the delirium of fever, and I realized that I must calm down and face the facts – grotesque as they were.

I was sufficiently acquainted with Moribundian diseases and phenomena generally to know that nothing which they would regard as unprecedented had taken place (I had indeed myself seen stranger things): but I had never dreamed that such a thing could happen to me. I had imagined, I suppose, that because I was human I was immune from Moribundian contagion of this sort. The only thing to do now was to find some remedy. I asked Mrs Juggins to call in a doctor as soon as possible.

The doctor came along during the morning, but, after giving me a brief examination, took the gloomiest view.

'No,' he said, shaking his head. 'This looks like one of those cases which defy all medical treatment. You may suffer agony for years.'

Angered by the defeatism of the man, I asked him no further questions, and he left me.

All the other doctors I called in told me the same thing, and there began for me a long period of agony and frustration, worse than anything I have ever known. It has been my fate, in this world, to have been in my berth seasick for as long as ten days on an ocean liner; and I once severely fractured my leg and was tied up motionless for eight weeks to that crude and sinister surgical invention – the 'Balkan Beam'. But such experiences, with the awful boredom they entailed, the dreary counting over of every minute and hour, were as nothing compared with this abominable confinement by heavy chains to my bed in a wretched little room in a Moribundian working-class district. Indeed, if I had taken the doctors at their word, and if I had not known that release fairly shortly awaited me – not death, but the *Asteradio*, being in this case the friend – I think I should have gone mad.

Much as I suffered from the pain of my cramped position and the shoots and stabs of the rheumatism itself, I think I can say it was the boredom which irked me most.

At an early stage I got Mrs Juggins to fix up a wireless in my room, and I listened in all day to the Moribundian broadcasts. But the pleasure of listening soon palled, and I was thrown back again on myself.

The only thing which remained to me were my books. I could still just manage to read, though I could only do this by getting Mrs Juggins to place the book in a certain position, inclining my head at a most painful angle, and turning each page by the motion of my little finger.

One day it occurred to me that, since there was no apparent remedy for me, and I had to suffer until Crowmarsh released me, I had better suffer heroically, and try and extract whatever benefit I could from this ironical imprisonment in a world to which I had come expressly for purposes of exploration and observation.

I perceived that the next best thing to seeing things was to read about them, and I made up my mind that, whatever the expenditure of pain and energy, I would methodically devour as much Moribundian literature of all kinds as I could possibly contrive to do in the time left to me. There was no shortage of books, for shortly after my arrival in Moribundia, I had paid my subscription as a member of the *Nwotsemaht* Library, a highly satisfactory institution which allowed me as many as fifteen books out at the same time, and which, if the member left a deposit (which I had fortunately already done), would send any book on receipt of a postcard.

Looking back on it now, I often think that my illness may have been a blessing in disguise, for in living up to this resolution of mine I read a huge number of books, and acquired a knowledge of Moribundian literature which I could not possibly have acquired in any other way.

At the outset I found that the pain and awkwardness of my attitude in bed were too great for me to read for too long stretches, however willing my spirit; but I succeeded in turning even this limitation to advantage. I conceived the excellent idea of committing to memory long passages from the various authors. This I was able to do when I was no longer physically capable of reading ordinarily. I had only to read a sentence, then lie back in a painless position to memorize it, and, when I had got it word perfect, go on to the next sentence and do the same.

Not only did this strenuous effort relieve my tedium, and make each day go by much more quickly than I could ever have hoped for; it enabled me, as I foresaw it would, to bring back with me to this world a collection of authentic passages and excerpts from actual Moribundian authors, correct in every word and phrase, as though I had brought back printed pages from the volumes themselves!

This is a feat of which I think I can be justly proud.

I have already, since my return, put down on paper many of these remembered excerpts, and I propose before very long to publish them all in a separate volume.

I shall probably then have some remarks to make about Moribundian literature, regarded purely as literature. In the meantime, I feel that this book would be incomplete if I did not make some general remarks on the subject, if only in its social and more superficial aspects, and will mark time by doing so in the next chapter – just as I had to mark time chained down on that wretched bed.

# CHAPTER SIXTEEN

For reasons which I shall be explaining, there was, up to the time I left, no actual censorship of letters in Moribundia, and so there was, seemingly, as great a diversity of style, opinion, and thought in their books up there as there is down here.

To give any idea of Moribundian literature as a whole, therefore, would require a volume or volumes, and anything I write here must be thought of, not as literary criticism, but as mere journalism. In a single chapter of this sort I can only offer a few brief remarks of a general nature, and give one or two hints or suggestions as to who are, or are becoming, the most popular writers up there, and (judging from these) as to what I take to be characteristically Moribundian literature.

That Moribundia *has* a characteristic literature there can be no doubt, but how to convey its quality to a worldly reader is indeed a problem.

I think my best course will be, first of all, to mention the three great names which, I think, completely lead the field up there – names which no pious Moribundian can think of without satisfaction, pride, and gratitude – the names of *Draydur Gnilpik*, *Ris Yrneh Tlobwen*, and *Nhoj Nahcub*.

Many successors and imitators of these three great men come to my mind, but their supremacy remains unchallenged, and I am sure that no one would dispute that, in the works of these three, Moribundia, and the Moribundian outlook generally, finds its richest, completest, fruitiest expression. Indeed, if we were not dealing with an ideal world, I should say that these writers were almost too good to be true.

What is it about these writers which places them head and shoulders above the others, which causes the true Moribundian, when reading them, to feel that his everyday feelings, his innermost thoughts, his remotest and most elusive ideals have been set down in immortal print?

I often think that we form our best judgment of a writer less from what he writes than from what he does not write: it is from what he leaves unsaid, from what he either unconsciously or adroitly assumes the reader to take for granted, that we glean his true quality. Such a method of appraisal is especially useful when dealing with these three writers, who, as though making a delicate assumption of the reader's breeding and integrity, leave a whole code of honour unsaid, and take a whole system of morals and politics entirely for granted.

What is this code of honour which is not mentioned, but which can be read between every line they write? Obviously the code of the *Akkup Bihas* – the great Moribundian ruling and administrative caste.

Again, it would require a separate volume to describe the *Akkup Bihas* in his completeness. I can only say here that he carries, in his full development, every quality of masculine idealism which I could see maturing in those wonderful boys who were playing cricket on the evening of my arrival.

I have a particular reason in mentioning that cricket match, for the early training of the *Akkup Bihas* in this game, and in the ethics of this game, is subtly but inextricably involved in the whole outlook, attitude, and even manner of the writers in question. 'To play with a straight bat' is a famous Moribundian phrase in regard to character and behaviour. It is also possible to *write* with a straight bat, and these three are Writers with a Straight Bat of a quality such as is not likely to be found again in time or space.

If I had room for it here I might trace the history of the Straight Bat in Moribundian literature from its earliest origins to the present time, seeking to discover the first, naïvest wielders of the implement. I might even begin some centuries back, and fancy I saw the spirit trying its wings in so small and long-distant a writer as *Lenoloc Ecalevol*, with his poem ending in the lines:

> *I dluoc ton evol eeht, raed, os hcum*
> *Devol I ton ruonoh erom**

after which I could trace the growth of the tendency through succeeding centuries to the last one, in which it climbs rapidly into maturity, being, every now and again, either furtively present or blazingly apparent in such widely divergent writers as *Elylrac*, *Nosynnet*, *Htiderem*, *Yarekcaht*, *Nosnevets*, even *Gninworb* … But I cannot pursue this here.

To return to the *Akkup Bihas*. Apart from this question of his early training on the cricket field, I should say that his other qualities comprise, above all, a love of arms, of duty, and of silence – this together with a sober joy in a kind of freemasonry binding each *Akkup Bihas* to his fellow, even if their interests are opposed and they are in actual physical conflict with each other.

Indeed, I sometimes think that this freemasonry is the most pronounced feature of the *Akkup Bihas* – the emotion which it inspires being carried to what would probably seem to us exaggerated lengths.

---

* Roughly 'I could not be so purely fond of you, my darling, if I were not a man's man and fonder still of fighting'.

In one of *Yrneh Tlobwen's* most vivid and stirring poems, or, you might say, in one of his most glorious hits to the boundary off his straight bat, we find him speaking of the ideal:

> *Ot ruonoh, sa uoy ekirts mih nwod*
> *Eht eof taht semoc htiw sselraef seye.*

which means, literally:

> *To honour, as you strike him down*
> *The foe that comes with fearless eyes.*

or, freely translated, 'to see, at the moment of conflict, whether your antagonist is an *Akkup Bihas* like yourself, and if he is, to show the greatest deference for his courage even while you are hitting him so hard that he falls down'.

Presumably the foe who is stricken down in this encounter is sensible of the same pure emotion, and such an attitude, adopted by either side in the heat of battle, is a feat of disinterestedness (and, indeed, Henry Cotton-like mental concentration at the moment of impact) which the non-Moribundian may hardly be able to understand, but which is a perfect example of the profound homage which each *Akkub Bihas* keeps in his firm, quiet breast for his equals.

These three writers have portrayed the *Akkup Bihas* in all phases of his life – at school, at his games, at war, in remote lands – and under the spur of all emotions. It is *Nhoj Nahcub*, however, who furnishes the fullest, simplest, most charming and unassuming pictures of the *Akkup Bihas* in everyday life, as a lawyer, an M.P., an explorer, a soldier, etc., either at his club or at his country house – giving us countless little details about his muscles, his bones, his figure, the colour and quality of his eyes and the effect of the climate upon his skin, which brings him life-like before our eyes.

The secret of the popularity and priority of place of these three in Moribundian literature cannot be attributed alone to their success in depicting the psychology, emotions and physique of the *Akkup Bihas*. Here, as everywhere else, the old Moribundian question of Change, or rather Changelessness, exerts its influence. It is not only that the (to Moribundians) impure thought of radical change has never in any guise sullied a line of their works: their whole fire, tendency, and literary skill (which is very great) are thrown into the service of the other cause – the burning portraiture of the ideal nature of the existing state of social affairs and class domination, the painting of it in those rich, glowing, ineffable hues which the less-inspired Moribundian may not have been able to discern, or, grown stale, may have forgotten – the revelation of the beauty, for all, of living in Moribundia, and the duty, for all, if need be, of dying for it. The wickedness and horror of the notion of any alteration of such a world is thus given by implication. It is as such that these three men (Moribundia being what it is and feeling what it does) take on the character of great teachers or seers, are, in fact, what I should call Moribundia's Holy Men, along with the two great exponents of political astronomy, *Snaej* and *Notgnidde*.

So much for the big three. I am tempted here very much to give some attention to the many smaller writers in the same vein, the candidates for the same laurels, who strive after the big manner without quite having the literary skill or taste to capture it. I should like to say something, for instance, of *Nai Yah*, *Nerw P. C.*, *Treblig Uaknarf*, *Yhtorod Srejas*, '*Reppas*', etc. – in fact, all the other diligent popular portrayers of the same type and outlook: but space does not permit, nor are their literary merits of a high enough order or of lasting enough a quality to warrant discussion in a brief resume of this sort.

I have spoken so far only of those authors whose whole outlook is in brimming accord with the Moribundian outlook. The reader may be now wondering whether, in such a world, any other sort of writer is allowed to exist or finds any readers. Soon after I began my studies, I made it my business to find out whether this was so or not, and I was at first amazed by what I discovered.

This brings us to the question of censorship in Moribundia. As I have said, I found out that there was no actual censorship of any sort where literary works are concerned. Anybody could write whatever he wanted to write; though whether he was read was another problem.

In view of the defensive and necessarily ruthless attitude of the Moribundians towards Change, this came as a great surprise to me, and bewildered me very much – especially as I soon came across various books, and highly popular books at that, which seemed to me to be expressing what would seem to be, from the Moribundian standpoint, decidedly audacious, if not definitely subversive, opinions.

The mystery was, indeed, solved at last, but not until I had made an extensive study of the authors in question, and obtained a proper view of them and their literary records as a whole. I can best exemplify this apparent contradiction by mentioning the works of two widely-read authors – *Dranreb Wahs* and *Trebreh Egroeg Sllew* – who, in a curious way of their own, hold a position in Moribundian literature second only to that held by the great three.

Now, whatever else may be said about these two, their influence upon the minds of their own generation has been colossal, and the covers of their books are crammed with controversial matter in which the hypothesis of Change is being brought forward shamelessly again and again. How can their popularity in Moribundia be reconciled with these facts?

This for a long time remained a mystery with me, until it began slowly to dawn upon me that the Moribundian authorities, in this matter of censorship, were a good deal wiser, more cunning and more patient than we are. That an eye had been kept from the beginning upon the writings of Messrs. *Wahs* and *Sllew*, I have no doubt. I also have no doubt that there must have been a strong temptation from time to time to suppress them utterly. Such, however, was not the Moribundian policy; the authorities, in their far-sighted wisdom, must have known always what it took the public years to discover, that is, that there was nowhere any deep-seated thought or love of really deep-seated change lurking behind the highly-readable polemics of these two, and that time would expose the unreality and irrelevance of their teachings. How justified they were time proved up to the hilt, as I was able myself to see when I read their works as a whole, and in chronological relation to changing events.

In fact, the truth of the matter is that cunning Moribundia, so far from discouraging, looks with the utmost complacence upon public figures of this sort, knowing that a very high propaganda value can be extracted from the spectacle of their slow disintegration before facts, and their virtual reabsorption into the camp against which they once seemed to rebel. Anything more tragic, hollow, and helpless than their present state of muddle and intellectual inadequacy in face of modern events could not be imagined, and so yet another, and unusually cogent, example is given to the man in the street of the fate awaiting those who call into question the changeless character of an ideal world.

Knowing these things, Moribundia, in cynical security, can afford to forget the grudge, and so in the course of time these writers begin to lose their black character and take on an almost lovable one, even amongst the most loyal and strait-laced Moribundians. They have shown themselves to have been bees that have stung without wounding: they have shown that there is no wound in the sting of all the other and lesser and future bees. Can one be surprised that, for making that most exhilarating demonstration, their indiscretions are gratefully forgiven, and that they at last gain a popularity which has in it something closely akin to affection?

I do not say that this is the only reason why these two may be called, in the proper sense of the term, characteristically Moribundian authors or why they are so popular as such. In the case of *Sllew*, for instance, the service paid to orthodox Moribundia goes a good deal deeper, and is often quite direct. He never, for instance, when he gets a chance, fails to please the pious Moribundians by getting in a dig at that hell-on-Moribundia I have mentioned – *Ehtteivosnoinu*: whereas his hatred of the arch-anti-Moribundian – *Xram* – reaches such fantastic proportions and takes such incredible outlets, that he would, on this score, alone, be forgiven all his sins against the light.

How deeply he must have felt on this subject is shown by the ill-concealed bitterness of his attack – by no means usual with him. Indeed, for the most part his writings are signalized by a sort of paternal and very grown-up equability towards everybody and everything, this being expressed in a warm, caressing, almost love-making style, which always makes me think of him, indeed, as a sort of universal Umpire in mankind's schoolboyish cricket match – an umpire being incessantly asked whether or no certain political systems or ideas are 'out' and generally being forced to give an adverse verdict in a kindly way. Even if they are 'not out' the first time, the dismissal is pretty certain to fall a few overs later. (He turns out books almost weekly.)

Another reason why the shrewder Moribundians are able to see that *Sllew* is at heart one with them, is, I think, the complete vacuum in which he writes – the total separation of his ideas from concrete and developing things as they are, his perfectly Moribundian belief in one sweet, absolute, unchanging Reason existing apart from facts – (yet hypothetically able to govern them) – an absolute reason whose formulas he, and a few others, are able to expound. But by a meaningless accident of time these secrets have remained concealed to past ages and one is forced to the conclusion that if only by a fluke *Sllew* had come on the scene earlier, and if only people had *read* him and done what he had told them to do when he *had* come, there would never have been any trouble. As things are, the next best thing is to read him and do what he tells us now.

This attitude is manifest in nearly all the other Moribundian writers I read, even those who (like *Dnartreb Llessur*, for instance) are for the most part irreconcilably hostile to the general Moribundian spirit, and who only by virtue of this 'vacuum-morality' can be styled in any sense Moribundian writers.

When I speak of a 'Moribundian' writer I mean, of course, one who in greater or smaller degree allies or associates himself with the changeless ideal of ideal changelessness on which Moribundia is founded, and as it is a question of degree I often had difficulty in ascertaining whether a writer might be termed 'Moribundian' or not.

This was particularly so when I came to make some appraisement of the younger or middle generation of intellectual writers. There are, of course, amongst these many easily discerned

Moribundians, arch-Moribundians indeed – that is, avowed wor-shippers of the static (like *Toile S. T.* and his followers), but there are also plenty of what seemed to me border-line cases. How was I to classify, for instance, writers like *Ecyoj, Yelxuh, Ecnerwal, Llewtis, Sevarg, Noossas,* etc.?

I have mentioned these names at random, but they all qualify in my opinion as authentic Moribundian writers, in spite of the fact that they are all on the surface rebels. They seem to me to be what they are because they have no other choice. This brings me to the whole question of literature in a changeless world.

I think any worldly critic of these writers would agree that they are for the most part hopelessly and morbidly turned in upon themselves, and sterile in consequence. But where else are they to turn save upon themselves? In a world which is unchangeable and inexpandible, where is there to gaze save inwards? Obviously, if they are to look anywhere, they must look through the micro-scope, all the horizons for the telescope being closed: obviously, in doing so, they must become self-conscious to an ever more tormented degree, and paralysed for effective action accordingly. Finally, a stage must be reached when the mind can only look at ever-receding reaches of the mind, and an art on the border-line of madness or idiocy must be reached.

Satisfying as the spectacle must be to true Moribundians, there is nothing more painful for one of our own world than to see a subversive intellect of, say, the *Yelxuh* type, beating round and round and driving itself to self-examining distraction in a world which has exhausted its possibilities of change – going on and on until it seems certain at last that it must throw itself upon that piteous act of faith which alone can put it out of its pain and bring it back to the piously Moribundian point from which it started.

For these reasons art, literature, and poetry in Moribundia

take on a more and more painfully subjective aspect, more and more the character of meaningless masturbation, there being no future which they can fertilize.

There are, of course, exceptions to this rule, writers and poets who flatly deny the whole Moribundian teaching with regard to change and development: but they are, naturally, either ignored or regarded as eccentrics and *poseurs*.

I repeat, then, that the writers I have mentioned, and the many others like them, may not inaccurately be described as Moribundian writers, for even those who have not already made the act of faith in question seem certain to do so in the near future, seem inevitably on their way to becoming Moribundian good boys, going to Moribundian Church, even if they fail to turn up in nice, clean collars.

With regard to the rest of the Moribundia writers, hardly any problem arises. There is, up there, as down here, a vast army of writers simply writing to please a public and make money. Such writers are 'Moribundian' in so far as they are forced to please a Moribundian public, but ordinary love stories, and detective stories and adventure stories are turned out on a changeless pattern in any world.

I am not going to say that there are not many in-between cases – lesser-known writers who are fully Moribundian, famous writers who are only half or not at all Moribundian, but it is quite beyond my scope to deal with them here. I have attempted in this chapter merely to show how the land lies and to give some idea of the sort of critical task which awaits this world when it comes to appraising the quality of the literary work of another. And it will have to come to that sooner or later – for this concrete world is coming to grips with that ideal one.

# CHAPTER SEVENTEEN

One morning Mrs Juggins came into my room, and told me that a friend of hers had a husband who had been chained to his bed, exactly like myself, for a period of many years, but had recently had a wonderful recovery by taking a dose or two of certain salts, whose name she mentioned.

I was in such misery and despair that I hardly listened to what she said, and when, the next day, she brought me in a tin of these salts – 'Banishill' Salts they were called – and gave me a dose, it was only to humour her that I was prevailed upon to take it.

What followed surpassed even Moribundian belief. With the first dose I began to hear a great cracking and splitting noise going on inside me, and this, Mrs Juggins informed me, was caused by the 'agonizing acid crystals' breaking up in all my joints – after the next dose my chains fell away from me and I sprang from the bed. With the third dose I was feeling better than I have ever felt in my life. My colour and appetite returned, and I had an extraordinary feeling of regeneration in all my limbs.

In fact, in the first glory of my relief from my illness, I am afraid I must have made something of a fool of myself, for I went about hitting people on the back, jumping or vaulting over everything that I could see, grinning from ear to ear (my very mouth seemed to have expanded and my eyes and teeth to have grown unnaturally large) and generally behaving in a way not at all suited to my age.

In my new happiness I was not so ungrateful as to forget its cause, and I even, I remember, wrote a letter to the makers of this wonderful remedy, putting my name and address at the top, explaining the facts exactly as they were – that is, that it had been a case which had seemed to defy all remedies, that all the doctors had given me up, that I had looked forward to suffering years of agony, etc., and adding that I would have no objection, if they wished, to the use of my name as a testimonial. In all the circumstances I felt that this was the least thing I could do.

They say that misfortunes never come singly, and I suppose the saying is true of good fortune. Certainly this was evidenced in my case at this time, for within three days of my recovery I had another stroke of wonderful luck, which immediately changed my whole outlook and circumstances.

I happened to see a small crowd waiting outside a church one morning, and, suspecting that a wedding was taking place inside, I waited in the hope of seeing the bride and bridegroom. In due course, they came out, the bridegroom looking wonderfully pleased with himself, and the bride, in her wedding dress, radiantly beautiful and happy.

It was after they had got into the taxi which was waiting for them, and while they were being driven away, that I happened, by the merest chance, to catch, through the window, certain balloons issuing from this handsome couple.

The first of these, from the man, was only what one might have expected:

ALONE AT LAST! YOU ARE MY BRIDE, NOW, AND WAS THERE EVER SUCH A FRESH AND BEAUTIFUL ONE IN THE WORLD? GIVE ME ANOTHER KISS!

To which she returned:

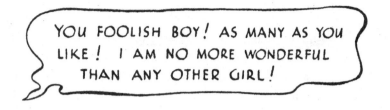

while from her head there came the 'thought-balloon':

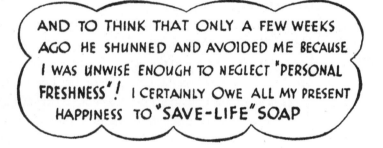

The taxi went round the corner and out of sight, and it was quite a minute before I realized that this last balloon might contain certain implications applicable to myself. Then suddenly I stopped in the street. 'Shunned and avoided?' Was not this what, inexplicably, Anne and everybody had been doing to me? 'personal freshness?' Had *I* been neglecting 'personal freshness'?

In a flash my whole misfortune was illuminated – Anne's coldness, her mysterious reticence, my unpopularity at the hotel, everything. Appalled as I was to think that I had been guilty of neglect of that kind, I realized, as soon as I thought about it, that it was in Moribundia a venal and very prevalent failing, and my joy knew no bounds to think that I had at last found the root of my trouble. Now I might return from my exile and see my dear Anne again!

I could hardly wait to act. I dived into the first chemist's shop I could find, and bought a cake of Save-Life Soap. The problem now was – where was I to have a bath? As all the bathrooms in this part of the world were used for storing coal, this was no easy matter. I quickly made up my mind that I would leave the district at once. I would, in fact, return to the 'Moribundian', itself, and have my bath there. During my illness I had saved up enough money to stay there for at least two weeks, and I felt I could not let a day pass before I saw Anne.

I went back home and hastily packed. I paid Mrs Juggins and thanked her for all her kindness to me while I was in chains. I asked her to say good-bye for me to the others, all of whom were out, and I left. I had not been treated badly there, but I was not sorry to see the last of that strange, despondent, destructive, indolent family, with its totally unnatural modes of thought and behaviour.

I was back at the 'Moribundian' by four o'clock in the afternoon, and was given my old room. Without waiting to unpack I tore off my clothes, seized the cake of soap, jumped into the bath, and stayed in it for something like an hour, emerging at last with a feeling of personal freshness exhilarating in the extreme. I then 'phoned to Anne.

She was, of course, most surprised to hear my voice, and I think I must have conveyed something of the freshness of my person even over the telephone, for she put up no obstacle, as heretofore, to our meeting. In fact, she agreed to come to dinner with me that night.

While I was waiting for her I found that the people in the hotel no longer shunned me. On the contrary, I seemed to magnetize them in a peculiar way, and was quite the centre of attraction. Indeed, more than once I found myself standing in the middle of a whole group of people, all of whom looked at me in a most admiring way as they listened to my conversation.

When Anne came round I, of course, presented her with a box of her favourite stockings, and over dinner we were as deliriously happy as on our first night together – tacitly agreeing to say nothing either about the long time we had been parted, or the cause of the break.

After my long illness and dreary isolation amongst the working people, it was an intoxication in itself to be amongst the bright lights and balloons again, and I felt that night that I could never tire again of this brilliant Moribundian scene. I have no doubt now, of course, that this was an illusion on my part, brought about by my sudden change of circumstances, and that in three days' time I should have been more heartily sick of it than ever. But no such knowledge marred my pleasure in that evening with Anne. Nor was I disturbed by any inkling or foreknowledge of something which would certainly have put an end to our gaiety, the fact that this was the last evening we should ever spend together, my last evening in Moribundia itself – that on the morrow it was fated that I should abruptly return to this world with all its different anxieties and cares.

# CHAPTER EIGHTEEN

I have spoken of Crowmarsh's 'fiddling' with the *Asteradio*, and of its effects upon me. Apparently it was similarly possible for me, under certain circumstances, to make the *Asteradio* itself aware, however faintly and obscurely, of my presence and activities, to cause it to react in certain ways which might inform the studious and vigilant scientist in Chandos Street that all was not well with me. Had this not been so I should not be here now: nor should I have still been in Moribundia: I would be dead. Crowmarsh, reading the Asteradial omens in his own way (I know no more about their precise nature than he knew precisely what was happening to me), saw that 'something was up', as he afterwards described it, and brought me back without delay.

There certainly was something up. But before I relate the adventures, or rather mis-adventures, of this next day, which very nearly destroyed me and brought me back from Moribundia eleven days before the arranged time, I have to tell the reader certain things which I have not had the occasion to mention before.

The first thing concerns Moribundia's ubiquitous Little Men, about whom – I fear inexcusably – I have not yet said anything.

Had I given any complete description of the Moribundian streets, restaurants, shops, or public places generally, I should not have failed to describe this remarkable race of dwarfs, who were to be seen everywhere, and were as much a part of the general scene as the balloons and other oddities.

They are not at all easy to depict to the reader. In trying to give a picture of the Moribundian *Yenkcoc*, it will be remembered, I mentioned the artist *Treb Samoht*. In very much the same way, in thinking of the Moribundian 'Little Man' there comes to my mind another great Moribundian artist, perhaps the greatest of all – *Eburts* – who has depicted this type so often, so skilfully, and with such loving care that, just as Dickens has been said to have invented Christmas, so he may almost be said to have invented the Little Man. If only I could have brought back some of his drawings I might have reproduced them here, and given the reader a more accurate picture than words can possibly do. But, unfortunately, Crowmarsh's service does not yet provide for the transportation of luggage between Moribundia and our earth!

The main features by which a Little Man can be recognized are his remarkable shortness and squatness, his moustache, his pince-nez, his bowler hat, and his umbrella. In fact, there is very little else about him, apart from his shortness, his moustache, his pince-nez, his bowler hat and his umbrella. It is certainly not a type which we on earth would admire. Indeed, resembling, as he does, the small sedentary business man, the petty trader or employer in his meanest, timidest, puniest, most conservative and insignificant aspects, the Little Man could only move a normal healthy human being to dislike or derision. I took it for granted, in my innocence, that the average Moribundian would feel the same. How mistaken I was, and the final result of my error, we shall see soon enough.

I remember how, on the very first walk I had with Anne, I began to notice these odd little persons, and how I asked her about them.

'Tell me,' I said, 'who are these silly little persons with bowler hats and umbrellas I see walking about everywhere.'

I remember she looked at me in a puzzled, incredulous way.

'Why,' she said, 'you don't mean our beloved Little Men, do you?'

And there was something scandalized in her look and tone which warned me that I was treading on dangerous ground, that in speaking thus, disparagingly of them I had committed an appalling breach of Moribundian good taste. I hastily contrived to change the subject.

This made such an impression on me that I was inspired thereafter to make other inquiries, though, of course, in a much more delicate manner, from other sources. To my utmost surprise, I found that so far from being objects of derision, the Little Men were regarded by all true Moribundians with a deep and loving homage amounting almost to religious devotion (a respect and devotion far surpassing even that which was accorded to the *Yenkcoc*), and that to breathe a word in their disparagement was to strike at the very core of the whole Moribundian ethical code.

Indeed, it became apparent that the Little Man, with all his little business-man's virtues – his submissiveness, his patience, his industry, his respectability, his wistful humour under difficulties, his intense and somewhat idiotic patriotism and loyalty to the throne, etc., was regarded as a pure and shining ideal – a symbol of all that every Moribundian, at his best, was or aspired to be.

I have said that after inquiries I found out about this attitude towards the Little Man: but I do not want to give the impression that I yet had any knowledge how deeply, irremovably imbedded, how jealously guarded, this instinct was in the heart of every Moribundian. Had I known that, I should never have made the mistake I did, and would not have been compelled to leave Moribundia in the odious and perilous way I did.

I will now leave the Little Men for a moment, and go on to tell of the other factor which contributed to my downfall from grace, my exposure as a complete alien, which came so suddenly and shockingly upon me that dreadful morning.

Shortly after my return from Seabrightstone with Anne (and before my loss of personal freshness had turned her away from me) I found her one day in a state of considerable anxiety about her brother, who had returned on leave from abroad (a place called *Aynek*) while we were away, and who had, owing to her foolishly having left some letters about, found out about her association with me, including the fact that we had been away together as man and wife.

I should here explain that Anne's brother had been to a Moribundian public-school and was an *Akkup Bihas*. Now it unfortunately happens to be the fact that one of the main emotions (if indeed it is not *the* main emotion) of the *Akkup Bihas* is his over-developed, you might say neurotic, anxiety and sensitiveness with regard to anything touching the private affairs or sex life of his sister. Indeed, the thought that she may have been treated in anything remotely resembling a dubious manner is enough to throw one of these highly-strung and slightly morbid fellows into paroxysms of pain and rage.

Well, it appears that Anne's brother had got it into his head that his sister had been wronged by myself (how far he was from the truth the reader knows well enough), and he had closed up into himself and was going about in a hardly balanced frame of mind. In fact, I could not help feeling sorry for the man, knowing what Moribundian nature is, and realizing that his particular nature could not allow him to feel otherwise. His condition was aggravated, too, I heard from Anne, by the fact that at this period he was suffering from personal trouble, having recently, in her words, 'walked out of a good woman's life' – a walk which an *Akkup Bihas* takes more than once in the course of his existence. With the two things combined, his general nervous condition must have been awful, and I offered to do anything I could to appease him. But Anne seemed to think this was out of the question.

The point was that the man was contemplating a physical assault upon myself: in fact, he evidently regarded such an assault as a moral duty. Since I could not meet him and talk to him reasonably, the only thing for me to do was to keep out of his way. This I successfully did, and was aided in my efforts, of course, by my loss of personal freshness, which exiled me for so many weeks, in a remote part of the town where he would never have dreamed of looking for me. But since my return I was naturally in the danger zone again.

Having now got over these somewhat tiresome explanations, I may come to my last day in Moribundia.

In view of what happened I was never to forget that morning, of course – but I think I should have remembered it even if it had not been signalized by my departure.

To begin with, it was a gloriously fine day, and directly I awoke I was aware of a feeling of wonderful gaiety and happiness in the air around me.

This impression was borne out by my first contact with another being. My chambermaid came bouncing into my room, unable to refrain from singing in her high spirits, and putting down my early-morning tea on my table with so jaunty an air that I might have regarded it as impudence had I not observed the light of some deep inner joy shining from her eyes. Seeing this, I readily excused her, deciding that she hardly knew what she was doing.

She had brought up a morning paper on my tray, and I had only to look at this to see what had happened.

## DAY OF NATIONAL REJOICING

was the head-line I saw sprawled across the front page, and I soon read on to discover that the Queen had very much earlier in the morning given birth to a baby!

I knew enough of Moribundia by now (and I hope the reader will, too) to understand that if one of its newspapers said that a certain day was a day of national rejoicing, then it would not be a day, as it would be in our own world, like every other day for ordinary people, but a day, as claimed, of national rejoicing, that is one in which joy reigned in the heart of every person in the nation.

My chambermaid, carolling and bouncing about at her work as she was, gave me only a mild foretaste of the high spirits which were to greet me as soon as I was dressed, and made my way down to breakfast. So joyful was the lift-man at the idea of another possible heir to the throne, that he could not refrain, having heard my bell and seen me through the bars, from roaring with laughter, and swishing humorously up and down from the top to the bottom of the hotel, three or four times, before letting me in. Then, cracking absurd, half-hysterical jokes all the time, he let me in and took me downstairs, and, of course, I tried to look as pleased as I could.

Then, when I reached the dining-room, all the guests were beaming with pleasure, shouting delightedly and informally to each other from table to table, and showing the utmost good-humoured patience with regard to the service which was, of course, slow, as the waiters, whistling and singing as they moved about, could not concentrate for laughter and elation on what they were doing, dropped plates about, and frequently stopped to juggle playfully with the knives and forks before placing them on the table. The manager, ordinarily a severe and scowling man, was looking on at all this with the greatest complacence. Soon after my arrival, he came up to me and slyly offered me a cigar, which, the moment I lit it, exploded in my face!

The poorness of the service, indeed, reminded me of another morning much earlier in my stay, when my newspaper had a very different story to tell. On this occasion the King had fallen ill with an attack of influenza, and the headline ran:

## NATION-WIDE ANXIETY

The misery, the apathy, the nervousness, the apprehensiveness, the sense of suspense showing on everybody's countenance and in everybody's behaviour that morning, had an even more disastrous effect upon the service than did this present elation. You could hardly get a servant to realize your presence, let alone answer you or do your bidding, so pale and thoughtful were they all. The lift-man, I recall, had such a miserable, wool-gathering appearance, was so utterly in the clouds, that I had to shout at him three times before I could make him realize that he was in a lift, and that it was his business to take me down. And the manager, when I asked him some question, turned round and nearly snapped my head off – apologising the next moment in abject tones which asked for, and clearly expected, my pity under the circumstances.

Not having any reason to rejoice myself, I soon found the atmosphere of the hotel was tiring me, and I decided to go round to the Club where I thought things might be a little quieter. This was my first mistake.

I should have remembered that Anne had told me that her brother, if and when he attacked me, would almost certainly do so outside my Club. I could hardly believe there was anything in this, but I could not shake her fixed idea that he would 'come down to my Club' – or 'haul me out of my Club'.

It seems that the *Akkup Bihas*, who naturally figures in several incidents of this kind in the course of his life, is moved by some Moribundian compulsion to ensure that they take place in the vicinity of a club – private houses, hotels, restaurants, cinemas, etc., being regarded by him as impossible backgrounds for the moral drama it is necessary for him to enact.

Unfortunately, I had forgotten all about this; indeed, it had completely slipped my mind that I was under the threat of attack. No sooner, however, had I reached the Club portals, and seen a good-looking, slightly-tanned young man standing against the railings, looking well dressed except for a horse-whip which he carried in his hand and which gave him an eccentric appearance, than the whole thing came back to me in a flash, and I realized that the moment had come when I would be called upon to defend myself.

There was not the smallest doubt it was Anne's brother (the facial resemblance alone told me that); and the fact that he advanced threateningly upon me the moment he saw me warned me that there was no chance of a peaceable settlement of our differences.

I flatter myself that I have the ability to think quickly in a crisis of this sort. I had, at once, and thankfully, taken in the fact that he was a good deal smaller than myself (otherwise I dare say I should have attempted to run away). I saw that I could knock him out without any difficulty if I only acted promptly enough, and it seemed to me that, for the benefit of both of us in the long run, and to terminate an intolerable situation at once, it would be wise for me to deliver a forcible blow which would put him out of action for some time.

Therefore, as he advanced upon me, I feinted with some skill, and landed a right-hand blow upon his jaw which immediately levelled him with the pavement, where he remained, not seriously hurt, but in a semi-conscious state.

This was my second mistake – not my worst, but very serious. It was here that I revealed for the first time my human, non-Moribundian nature in its extreme for all to see.

It must be understood that, according to Moribundian standards, I had to be in the wrong. We need not argue whether or not I had behaved in a questionable manner with this young man's sister. An *Akkup Bihas*, when he desires to knock anybody down outside a club, is automatically ethically in the right. What is more – so much is the spirit the master of the mind up there – it was *physically* impossible for such a one as myself (a *dac*, a *rednuob*, or *redistuo* as I would have been called) to defend myself against, let alone to strike down, an *Akkup Bihas* in such a situation. And yet I had calmly enacted the physically impossible!

If I had been exceptionally lucky no one might have seen me and I might have escaped the consequences; but my luck did not hold so far. Directly I had knocked the young man down, I looked round to see if the episode had been observed, and saw, on the other side of the road, one of Moribundia's Little Men, gaping at me in surprise, panic, and dismay.

Knowing the Moribundian psychology as I do, I can fully understand what he was feeling. He recognized the scene – one which must have been quite familiar to him. He was outside a club, and there was no mistaking which of us was the *Akkup Bihas* and which the *rednuob* – apart from everything else, the former's horse-whip was still clutched feebly in his hand. And yet here the whole order of nature had been reversed. By knocking the *Akkup Bihas* down I could not have startled the Little Man more if I had turned into a fish or a bird in front of his eyes. I had revealed myself as a monster, with immense and occult powers.

Now just at first I had no idea of what I had done, and was not inclined to bother about what the insignificant Little Man might be thinking of me. I did not think it advisable now to enter the Club, and I walked away from the scene in no particular direction.

When I had been walking about five minutes, and had quite cooled down again, I did happen to look back, however, and momentarily fancied I saw the Little Man following and watching me from a safe distance. But all the Little Men are so alike that I presumed it was probably another one, and that I was mistaken.

After a while I found the streets in which I was walking were becoming more and more filled with people, and I soon came into a wide thoroughfare where the crowd was lined up on either side, and through which a procession of some sort was evidently going to pass. On inquiring, I ascertained that the King would soon be passing this way, and that all were doubly eager to see and cheer him on this day of national rejoicing.

Glad of the opportunity to see him myself, I decided to wait with the rest. There were plenty of Little Men about in the crowd – there is nothing they like so much as a procession and they always turn out in great force on such occasions – and it would have been quite impossible for me to distinguish the one I had imagined was following me, even if I had tried to do so, which I did not. All the same, I believe he was there, and watching me closely.

After I had been waiting about five minutes, it happened that a band not far away struck up the tune of the Moribundian National Anthem. I did not, of course, know the tune, and as I was standing in the front row of the crowd I did not notice that all the people around me were removing their hats.

A moment later I felt my own hat being tilted over my eyes. I turned round quickly and saw that this had been done by the umbrella of a Little Man, who was standing behind me, and who had evidently thought he would remind me of my duty in this wistfully cheeky and humorous way – very characteristic of his kind.

I was, of course, furious, and, in my spite, stuck my hat more firmly than ever on my head. The next moment I felt a blow from behind, and my hat went flying out into the middle of the road, where it encountered the hooves of a policeman's horse and was crushed out of all recognition.

I was now too angry to think what I was doing. I turned round upon the Little Man responsible for the outrage, and with an exasperated 'What the devil do you mean, sir?' I snatched his own hat from his hand and threw it out into the middle of the road.

I began to walk away at once, but not before I had heard an astonished murmur, a sort of gasp go up from all those in the vicinity who had witnessed the incident. There was something in that sound – the sound of Moribundia outraged and stirring – which struck panic into my soul at once, although I would not admit it to myself and tried not to increase my pace too obviously as I moved away.

Seeing an empty side street I walked quickly down it, but the news of my deed had travelled faster than myself, and as I approached its other end, I saw, standing on the corner, a band of five or six Little Men, seemingly waiting about with nothing to do, yet watching me with an intent, cat-like, curiosity behind their pince-nez, which somehow held more terrors for my mind than I should have felt from any immediate or openly-shown hostility.

It would have been fatal to have withdrawn, so I went up to, and by them, with as good a face as possible, trying to look unconscious of any situation, and casting a cool, casual glance upon them as I passed; but they remained motionless, frozen, regarding me with the same cat-like stare.

I had now entered the next street, and had proceeded up it about twenty yards when I began to hear behind me the soft pad of little following feet (*their* horrible little feet!) and, looking ahead, I saw that another group of these frozen, menacing, nightmarish little creatures was awaiting me at the next corner.

This was certainly not the time for detached thinking, but I remember that it was at this moment that there first dawned upon me a full idea of the black and unforgivable nature of my crime against this world. Not only had I outraged physical and moral law by knocking down an *Akkup Bihas* (and I was somehow certain by now that the Little Man who had seen me do it had spread the news abroad): not only had I failed to remove my hat during the playing of the National Anthem: I had provoked, insulted and assaulted a Little Man himself. In other words, I had provoked, insulted, and assaulted Moribundia itself – the sacred figure which represented its dearest ideals and loftiest aspirations. What could await me now but a lynching as soon as I was caught?

Still pathetically trying not to increase my pace, I passed this second group of Little Men, and went down another side street. But I still heard the soft pattering of those little feet behind me, and at last I could bear it no longer and broke into a run.

If I had hoped to evade my pursuers by doing this, I could not have made a greater mistake, for the moment I began to run it seemed that Little Men sprang up from nowhere on all sides. Everywhere I looked I could see them. They were standing in the doorways, they blocked my path on the pavement and road, they were waiting at each corner, and from every distance and vista they seemed crowding and rushing towards me. It seemed that the entire population of Moribundia had assumed the form of the Little Man, and was after my blood!

Thinking back on it, I am not sure that this was not the case – I am not sure that the Moribundians, in a great crisis of this sort, when the utmost solidarity was called for, were not able to assume physically their ideal, characteristic form, and to give chase to me in the character of the Little Man of their dreams whom I had affronted. Such a thing would not be at all wonderful and incredible in such a world; and I certainly know this, that from the moment I began to run I, myself, saw nothing but Little Men – Little Men, it seemed to me, in their hundreds and hundreds of thousands.

And by this race of dwarfs I was hounded out of Moribundia! The memory of that pack, and that pursuit, is still too fresh in my mind for me to think of it without terror.

I have said that I began to run: and at that their numbers seemed to increase a hundredfold and they began to run after me. I burst into a sprint, and still more appeared from all sides and from all corners, rushing towards me, converging on me, like the rats of Hamelin or the Gadarene swine!

My only hope lay in my speed and size. They had no concerted plan of action against me, and so long as I was running my momentum and strength prevented them from attacking me effectively and getting me down. Some, bolder than the rest, flung themselves upon me, but they could not maintain their hold, and were sent spinning away; others I kicked out of the way, like so many absurd and protesting little footballs, as I ran. The air was thick with the umbrellas they threw at me from all sides, but which were too small to hurt me.

I knew that the moment I stopped running, the moment they got me to the ground, I was finished. But how was I to keep up this pace? Where could I hide, and where was I going now?

And now, psychologically, the weirdest thing happened. I found that I knew the answer to this last question. I was deliberately making for a street called *Sodnahc* Street – had subconsciously been making for this street all along. I have never been able to account for this. I had not, so far as I know, known even of the existence of this street before now and yet, all at once, it presented itself to my mind as a refuge, a possible means of escape, a contact with the *Asteradio* itself, with Crowmarsh himself. It was almost as though this *Sodnahc* Street was some mystical Moribundian reflection, or counterpart of that very Chandos Street in the West End, which Crowmarsh inhabited and whence my journey had begun!

But my sensations were by this time of so completely unreal and nightmarish a quality, that it is impossible to speak with any clarity about the matter. After that moment when I realized I had been subconsciously making for *Sodnahc* Street, I can remember practically nothing in detail.

I can remember a great wave of relief as I reached the street I was seeking; I can remember feeling there was something familiar about it, and I can remember (or think I can) bursting into a house on the left-hand side, with the Little Men, presumably, at my heels.

What the house looked like inside I do not know, but at

this point the clouds lift again. I can remember, quite clearly, seeing in front of me what I took to be a small lift, electrically lit and with a sliding iron grating in front of it – very much like the sort of lift you would see in a small hotel in London, one which the guests themselves work. I plunged into this and slid back the grating, which seemed to lock automatically. The next moment the Little Men were upon it, trying, ineffectually, to tear it down.

How they swarmed upon that grating, how they huddled and pressed forward, how they shook their fists and glared! The noise they made, the way they fought for a view of me, the way they tried to poke at me with their umbrellas!

I stood there, at the back of the lift, facing them – terror in my heart, for I knew that they must soon devise some way of breaking in. That was my last view of Moribundia, the last vision I had of the Moribundians, and what a vision it was!

It seemed, in those few moments that were granted to me at the end, that I was able to see and understand this world of Little Men as I had never seen or understood it before, that I was able, in the innumerable faces of these little creatures, in the many-headed monster now before my eyes and seeking to devour me, to perceive and read the soul of Moribundia itself – its inner thoughts and motives as opposed to its superficial appearances. And what I saw on those faces was not good. Instead of the harmless, helpful, friendly, tolerant, duty-doing little business men, it was given to me to see something quite different – all the qualities which the artist *Eburts* and his admirers were unable to see. I saw cupidity, ignorance, complacence, meanness, ugliness, short-sightedness, cowardice, credulity, hysteria and, when the occasion called for it, as it did now, cruelty and blood-thirstiness. I saw the shrewd and despicable cash basis underlying that idiotic patriotism, and a deathly fear and hatred of innovation, of an overturning of their system, behind all their nauseatingly idealistic postures and utterances.

That was how I thought of Moribundia – concentrated in, and symbolized by, the Little Man, with his mask off – at that moment. But it must be remembered that I was seeing what I was seeing under circumstances which would hardly lead me to take a favourable view, and my subjective state of mind must be taken into account.

At any rate, the moment was brief enough. Above the angry roar of those little voices I became aware of a humming, droning, hypnotic noise – something like the noise of an electric vacuum cleaner, something like a dentist's drill at the peak of its song.

I listened intently to this rhythmic sound, which seemed to be approaching nearer, and was seized by the hideous fancy that it came from some engine of destruction with which they meant to blow me out of my refuge. Then it grew nearer and nearer, and I found myself surrendering to its hypnotic quality, growing almost sleepy.

All at once I realized that the noise was coming, not from outside, but from within the 'lift' – from within my own ears! I closed my eyes. I opened them and saw, instead of the wild Little Men, a clear and shining image of myself in a mirror, staring in a puzzled way at myself. At the same moment the noise within my ears grew to an intolerable volume, and I understood everything. This was not, never had been, a 'lift'; I was in the *Asteradio* and I was on my journey home!

Almost immediately, instead of being grateful for my good fortune, for the miracle which had saved me, I was conscious only of anguish and terror, and felt that I would rather go back and die a thousand deaths at the hands of the Little Men than have to listen again to that awful noise, with that awful Knowledge behind it, which already, from an illimitable distance, I could feel moving in my direction. *Not again, not again, not again!* That was the thought that went through my tortured and desperate head as I braced myself, straining at the steel bands which bound me, to descend once more into the engine-room of the Universe!

I am glad to say that on that return trip I was spared a renewal of that experience. I was not taken down to the engine-room. I was merely given a friendly reminder of its existence by hearing it from afar. Or if I did go down I was not conscious while I was there. Unconsciousness was granted me at the moment I prayed for it and, except for a vague, dreamy memory I have of waking for about thirty seconds in the stifling heat and glare of the *Asteradio* (and feeling quite sure that owing to some mistake I had been inside it for about three months, and that I was certainly about to die), I did not regain consciousness until I had been flung back again on this earth.

The circumstances of my reappearance are too much a matter of common knowledge for me to relate in detail. As is known, error entered in, and instead of being taken out of the *Asteradio*, as was anticipated, like a piece of cake that had been put away in a cupboard, I was first found, hysterically sobbing, at one o'clock in the morning, on the steps of the Constitutional Club in Northumberland Avenue.

The constable who was called to me was unable to get anything from me. Apart from incessantly repeating the words 'For King and Empire, For King and Empire', I would not talk, and I could not get any clear idea of who I was, where I had been, or what I was doing.

I simply wept floods of tears and repeated the same words.

What caused my choice of these words I have no idea. I had at the time, as far as I can remember, a feeling that it was urgently necessary for me to deliver a solemn message or slogan of some sort (presumably from Moribundia) and these were the only words that came into my head. I was removed from the steps of the Constitutional Club to the Police Station. The whole thing was very odd.

At the Police Station I slept for three hours, and awoke with my memory unimpaired, and with a full knowledge of everything exactly as it had happened. I immediately demanded my freedom: but my story was not believed, and I created something of a disturbance. I was finally persuaded to wait until the morning, and the hours of waiting were not pleasant. Finding myself behind bars like this, and seeing the bland incredulity of the police, I was seized by the ugly fancy that perhaps Crowmarsh would disown me, that perhaps, even, there was no Crowmarsh and no *Asteradio*, that I was to be disowned, outcast, by this world as well as by the Moribundian, that I had no place in either – no place, that is, amongst the stars and the planets at all!

But after various irritating delays my identity was established, and at nine o'clock the next morning Crowmarsh himself did me the honour of coming round in a taxi to fetch me. I believe to this day that he was less worried about my state of health than about the error which had disabled him from taking me out of the *Asteradio* like a piece of cake out of a cupboard: but I was too glad to see him to be bothered about anything of that sort.

He was polite and charming, and at once took me back in the taxi to Chandos Street. Here, in his room on the ground floor (not upstairs, thank you!), he put me into an armchair and, early as the hour was, offered me a whisky and soda. I accepted the offer, and also had a cigarette. The reader, who will have had enough difficulty in believing much that I have told him, will readily take my word when I say that I have never enjoyed a drink and smoke so well, before or since.

And if a Moribundian balloon could have come out of my head as I sat in that chair, I am not dubious concerning the form it would have taken. It would have been, complacently:

THE END